FOOTSTEPS OF ANGELS

Empire builder Max Feyman had ruthlessly gained control of an invention called the 'zipdrive', a system of ultra-fast space travel. But his world is shattered when his daughter Celia, holidaying on the moon, is suddenly rendered unable to walk or speak — dependent on others to remain alive. Then, across the solar system, others are also struck down. Feyman must find a cure for the mysterious affliction that threatens not only the life of his only daughter — but also humanity itself!

E. C. TUBB

FOOTSTEPS OF ANGELS

Complete and Unabridged

LINFORD
Leicester

First published in Great Britain

First Linford Edition
published 2008

Copyright © 2003 by E. C. Tubb
All rights reserved

British Library CIP Data

Tubb, E. C.
    Footsteps of angels.—Large print ed.—
Linford mystery library
    1. Epidemics—Fiction
    2. Science fiction
    3. Large type books
    I. Title
    823.9'14 [F]

    ISBN 978–1–84782–189–8

Published by
F. A. Thorpe (Publishing)
Anstey, Leicestershire

Set by Words & Graphics Ltd.
Anstey, Leicestershire
Printed and bound in Great Britain by
T. J. International Ltd., Padstow, Cornwall

1

They were the favored of fortune; young, spoiled, rich. The heirs of established wealth which cocooned them in a safe, snug, well-ordered world, their happiness marred only by the threat of boredom. Free to do as they pleased some made bizarre choices. The latest was to zip the sun.

'He's mad.' Celia Feyman moved to the window to stare at the bleak grandeur of the Moon. 'He'll never make it. It's suicide. He should be stopped, Aldo.'

'By whom?'

'You could talk to him. Use your influence.'

'And spoil the event?' Fabrizi shook his head and joined her at the window. 'I've talked to him,' he admitted, 'but who am I to say that he's wrong? And even if I was certain he would fail what difference would it make? Paolo has made up his mind. He's going to zip the sun.'

Following how many who had tried it before him? Too many, she guessed, and like the others he would never be seen again. Everything was against it; the math, the physics, the basic logic of the thing. And, most of all, the sun itself. The ravening atomic furnace waiting in space to convert Paolo and his ship to a puff of incandescent vapor.

'There's nothing we can do,' said Fabrizi and she felt the touch of his hand as it circled her waist. 'Other than to wish him luck, of course. Will you do that?'

'Of course. Now?'

'Later.' His hand rose a little higher towards the swell of her breast. 'We have plenty of time.'

'But not for that.'

She turned, breaking free, moving away to halt in the center of the room to face him where he stood against the window. A man inches taller than herself, smoothly formed, his skin a deep olive, his eyes liquid, his movements holding a cat-like grace. At twenty-two he was slim, taut, proudly masculine.

'Celia?'

'Nothing.' She was no prude, no stranger to sex or passion, and she had liked him from the first. Enough to have accepted his hospitality knowing what it implied. 'I'm sorry, Aldo, but — '

'You are thinking of Paolo, I understand.' If disappointed he hid it well. 'But we are on holiday. Here to enjoy what Luna has to offer. After Paolo has left we shall dine and visit the gardens. We could swim a little or dance or go sledding or zip to Kepler. We could take a crawler and examine the rays. As for the rest — ' His shrug was eloquent. 'It will be as you decide.'

It had been that since she was twelve, eight years ago now, and she saw no reason to change. But Aldo had been kind and she closed the gap between them, hands extended, head craning forward as she closed their lips in a kiss.

As it ended she said, 'Let's go and wish Paolo luck.'

He was not alone. Everyone in Tycho it seemed had come to look at the man who hoped to push back the frontiers of knowledge or the nut who had chosen a weird way to die. Which depended on the point of view; Paolo was both, but he was obviously enjoying his moment.

Celia studied him as she and Fabrizi moved closer. He stood on a dais at the end of the chamber leading to where his vessel waited outside. A smooth and smiling man, one too young to be tired of life, too old to have the unthinking confidence of a child. Too rich to be stopped and too handsome to be wasted. A man who radiated the excitement that dominated him, the euphoria born of what he was about to do.

Prometheus daring to snatch secrets from the sky — Celia hoped he would have a different fate.

'Can you tell me what you hope to achieve?' The voice was nasal, emanating from a big man carrying a recorder. A newshound after material. 'Everyone knows the zipdrive can only move a ship forward at about ten thousand miles a pulse. To penetrate the sun will take at least eighty pulses. How do you hope to survive?'

A good question and Celia strained to

catch the answer. The problem was obvious to a schoolboy; the moves weren't long enough and Paolo would approach too close then would actually emerge within the sun itself. Why was he being such a fool?

'Your name, sir?' Paolo nodded as the questioner gave it. 'Well, Mister Calton, I assume you know how the zipdrive works. A pulse is generated and the field and the vessel embraced in it is displaced from one point to another. You understand? The ship does not move — it is displaced. The difference is important. It means that a ship can penetrate any barrier because it does not actually move through it. How this happens is not as yet fully understood but it does and that is good enough.'

'So?'

'In a zipship you have the impression of continuous movement. Computers take care of the triggering and modulation of the pulse so that by a back and forth displacement you get just where you want to go. The same computers make certain you can't emerge within a solid object. The pulse itself is of short duration and can be varied within certain limitations. In actual fact we achieve a working velocity of a twentieth the speed of light. Is that perfectly clear?'

'I appreciate the lecture but you haven't answered the question. The sun is about five light seconds in diameter. That means you'll be a hell of a time inside. About two minutes, right?'

'Normally, yes. The journey would take that long.'

'How are you going to stop getting burned?'

'Because I won't actually be within the sun.' Paolo's voice betrayed his impatience. 'The ship is displaced — not moved. You talk as if I'll be driving through the sun.'

'But you'll emerge within it.'

'No.' Paolo took a deep breath. 'Not actually. The computers wouldn't let me get close unless they were reprogrammed which they are. What I intend to do is to use three generators in sequence. As one zip ends another pulse is generated before the first has fully died. They overlap, so to speak. The third generator is for emergencies.' Paolo lifted a hand to end the interview. 'No more now. I don't want to give away any secrets. See me again after I've zipped the sun.'

The rest was anticlimax. Of edging forward and touching his hand and wishing him luck as all the others were doing. Of waiting until his ship lifted in a zip that took it from view. Of waiting, and waiting, and waiting.

Of finally accepting that Paolo had failed.

'He had his moment.' Fabrizi lifted his glass in a toast to a man who had tried to do too much. 'And he did as he willed.'

Celia joined him as he drank. Paolo was gone, now a memory, yet it was hard to think of the living, breathing man she had seen as now a coil of vapor. What must it have been like? The waiting, the tension, the mounting excitement, the final fear when, too late, he had known he was wrong. Yet death must have come quickly, so quickly that he need never have known. A kindness and she drank with a lighter heart as she thought about it.

'Aldo?'

'Yes?'

'Let's have fun.'

A shift of mood, euphoria generated by the propinquity of death, one he took advantage of glad that she had ceased to brood. Tycho held a variety of delights and he took pleasure in guiding her around.

'Beautiful!' She stared at blooms of glowing intricacy and monstrous size housed in the regulated environment of deep-dug caverns. A forest of orchids tended by deft gardeners. 'Aldo! I never guessed!'

As she had known little about the pool with water tinted to a violet shade, streaked with metallic colors that crawled over her naked flesh to create transient patterns of enhancing loveliness.

Or the slides down which she plummeted to be slowed and spun and sent hurtling again in a long, twisting, stimulating journey through transparent tubes hugging the side of a crater wall.

The soaring edifice which gave a magnificent view of the rays stretching from the crater itself and which had made

Tycho both mysterious and enticing long before men had learned to fly.

A crevasse which contained a enigmatic construction which could have been the bulk of an ancient, time-distorted vessel or an accidental fabrication or the happenstance of weathering but which caught at the imagination and made her feel suddenly very small and very vulnerable to the hostile forces of the cosmos.

Then back to the hotel to nibble at succulent dainties and sip at foaming drinks glowing blue and amber, emerald and ruby, tasting the bittersweet blend of herbs, the tang of alien ice.

'You like it?'

'I love it.'

'And me?'

'I love you too.' She reached out to send her fingers tracing a path over his cheek. 'Aldo. Dear Aldo.'

They danced and he felt the softness of her against him before the music had them part to gesticulate, to weave an intricate saraband, to meet again in formalized abandon. A game which merged with the other they played, the old game of love and being in love. One both had played before and would play again many times and, when the time for parting came, neither would have regret.

'A toast!' A woman rose at the edge of the floor, tall, regal, her skin black, her hair, gown, shoes, teeth a gleaming white. The drink in her hand was the color of blood. 'To a hero! To Paolo!'

The end of the wake and Celia joined the others who buried his memory. Fabrizi caught her as she stumbled.

'Celia?'

'I'm high.' She smiled at him. 'Too high. Get me something to bring me down.'

Tablets to neutralize the alcohol while leaving the exhilaration. To those who could pay pleasure need hold no pain.

Back in their suite she spun, arms lifting, her figure reflected against the panes of the window. Double-glazing beyond which lay the vacuum of space and the harsh bleakness of the lunar terrain. Looking at it she sensed the age of the fretted stone, the pocked craters, the leached and weathered peaks and mounds. Formations which seen from a distance resembled the contours of a skull. An association too closely aligned with death and she moved from the window to spin again like a luminous ghost against a vista of stars.

'Celia!' Aldo stared his admiration. 'You look like an angel.'

She wore white to match the silver of her hair; silk edged with gleaming metal, the gown arranged to leave one shoulder bare, the material enhancing the nacreous pallor of her skin. It fell with a rustle of fabric to lie in a mound on the carpet as, nude, she reared, stretching, arms lifted as if to grasp some unattainable object.

'Aldo!'

His arms closed around her, lifted her, carried her to the wide bed. Black sheets threw her whiteness into a radiant splendor the ebon pillow laced with the tresses of her hair. A woman, young, spoiled, rich, demanding his attention, his love.

'Aldo! Aldo!'

'Celia! My darling!'

A time of storm, during which the universe shrank to the parameters of the bed. A period of trusting surrender and mutual compliance followed by a blissful tranquility.

In the calm she looked at the window, the scene it framed, seeing dancing flickers illuminate the panes with random brightness. Beside her Aldo stirred.

'Celia?'

'Hush.'

'What are you looking at?'

'The footsteps of angels.' She smiled, not looking at him. 'Isn't that what you called me? An angel? Well angels must have feet and I'm looking at the marks those feet would make.' She gestured at the window. 'See?'

He frowned, then understood. 'Those lights? They're from the zipships.'

'Don't spoil it.'

'But it's true. They are reflections from the field and — ' He broke off, aware that he had been too factual. 'Sorry.'

'It doesn't matter.'

'You're sensitive.' His hand reached to touch her own. 'I should have known.

You've written poetry and, well — forgive me?'

'I'll try.' She stretched, glad to be alive, feeling the demands of her body as his proximity triggered an ancient response. 'Aldo!'

'A moment.' He was hot, conscious of recent sweat, aware of potential body-odor and unwilling to neglect elementary hygiene. 'I'll just grab a shower and freshen up. Need anything?'

'No.'

'A drink?'

'Just you beside me.'

'I won't be long.'

'Promise?'

'I promise.' He saw her look at him, the movements of her eyes, her smile. 'I love you, darling.'

And thought he meant it as he stepped into the shower. He did mean it, for now at least, and what was eternity but the endless extension of a moment? Life with Celia could be good, perfect if their love could last, but to ask that was to ask for too much. Better to settle for less. For what he had now. To enjoy it and let the future take care of itself.

As the water lashing his body took care of its cleanliness. As the pills he swallowed took care of his fatigue. As the lotion he carried in a small flask took care of the flat taste in his mouth and scented his breath as it tingled against his palate and sent warmth to his loins.

'Darling.' He returned to the bedroom primed and ready for love. 'Are you awake?'

She lay as he had left her, sprawled on the wide bed, nude, the long, silver tresses of her hair gracing the pillow as her skin glowed against the sheets. A long-legged, well-made, beautiful woman who remained silent as he called, motionless as he touched her.

'Darling. Don't play games with me. Dar — my God!'

Celia lay before him, alive, breathing, warm, a woman to be used or abused, a lovely shell framed like a pearl in an ebon setting. But Celia, the woman who had smiled at him, talked and laughed with him, whispered to him and told him of her love — that woman had gone.

2

Once the clinic had been a hunting lodge set among pines and backed by mountains crested with eternal snows. A secluded place which provided a convenient refuge for the sick and dying, for those needing unorthodox surgery as well as those needing the best medical care money could obtain. Time had expanded it into a complex of wards and private rooms, of operating theaters, of rooms stuffed with the latest equipment. Its reputation was of the best. Doctor Evan Ganter wanted to keep it that way.

He was a tall man, smoothly elegant, neatly dressed. His eyes were brown, his hair gray, his hands those of an artist. Cheeks, throat and jowls bore the sheen of expensive care. A man at the height of his profession accorded deference and respect from his staff and patients alike. The smile he wore was designed to convey a warm and comforting reassurance.

To Feyman it was the grimace of a ghoul.

He said, harshly, 'Well?'

'Please be seated.' Ganter waved to a chair in his office. One his visitor must have been offered before and had refused it then as he did now. 'Would you like something to drink, Max? Coffee and brandy, perhaps?'

'To hell with that. What about Celia?'

Ganter retained his smile. It was natural for a father to be concerned about his daughter. Especially when she was his only living child. When she had no mother, When he was so rich.

'There has been little progress,' Ganter admitted. 'But there are no signs of further deterioration. The latest series of tests might be able to tell us something new and there are several things I'd like to try once the results have been assessed.'

'Experiments?' Feyman shook his head at the doctor's gesture. 'Forget it. No one uses my girl for a guinea pig.'

'No one will.' Ganter was quick with his assurance. 'But you must be rational about this. Without a firm base of knowledge on which to work anything we attempt must be in the nature of an experiment. Each drug we try is a gamble; we are certain it will cause no harm but we can only hope it will provide a cure. It's a matter of trial and error. We could be lucky the very first time or — '

'How long?'

'For what?'

'Damn it, man, you know what I mean. How long do you have to keep trying?'

He meant how long until the girl died and Ganter wondered why the man found it so difficult to put into words. A mental block, maybe, the fear that if he gave voice to the thought he would also give it substance and so turn a concept into reality. A superstition Ganter had met before and one he ignored. Feyman had demanded the truth and he would get it as far as it could be given.

'I don't know.' The admission brooked of no argument. 'Any estimate I made would be based on pure speculation. We have so little to work on. But I am optimistic. As far as we can determine she is in no immediate danger. The autonomic nervous system is maintaining essential functions; heartbeat, respiration, eye-lid movement, balance, basic mobility. Movement when resting and asleep,' he explained. 'Turning and shifting so as to avoid clotting of the blood. The autonomic system takes care of basic survival. As for the rest, well, how can I put it?'

A question posed for effect but Feyman already had the answer.

He said, 'She doesn't seem able to see. To hear. To feel. To be aware that anyone is with her. She doesn't talk. She doesn't respond. She's no more than a damned vegetable.' He looked at his hands, the fist they had made. 'When I was young we had a name for people like that.'

'Such as?' Ganter waited but again the block held Feyman silent. 'Crazies?' he suggested quietly. 'Nuts? Idiots?'

'Celia is — '

'None of those things. I know. Neither is she a spastic or autistic and, remember, neither of those types are crazy in the accepted sense of the term. They are the

18

victims of a poor mental and physical coordination coupled, in some cases, with a temporal displacement.' Psychic traumas that made a cure impossible but Ganter didn't mention that. No doctor should ever confess to inadequacy. 'But don't worry,' he said. 'Celia is having the best of care.'

'Will it cure her?'

'The care alone, no.'

'She can get care at home. What can you give her I can't?'

'Max, you're upset and concerned and maybe a little disappointed and I understand how you feel. But the main object of concern must be Celia. Here she is under constant observation. We are giving her top priority. She has the best of medical attention and the benefit of the latest techniques and equipment.'

'But she could still die?' Feyman pressed the point. 'Despite all your skill and care and equipment my girl could still die. Right?'

A hard man with hard questions and not one to be easily smoothed: or satisfied. Yet Ganter did his best.

'We're doing everything we can, Max.'

'Which means what? Can you guarantee to save her?'

'No one can do that. People die all the time.'

'Without cause? You've had her here six weeks now and what have you learned?' Feyman stared at the doctor hating what he saw. A ghoul, worse, a failure. A creature battening on the pain and suffering of others. The neat hands were stained with blood, the clothing a rotting shroud, the hair and expensively tended skin masked a grinning skull. And he had reason to grin; while people paid him for taking care of their problems he had it made. 'I want to see my girl.'

'That would be unwise.' Ganter was quick with his objection. 'You would only upset yourself. Just remember that you're doing all that can be done,'

Feyman said, flatly, 'I disagree. Now take me to my daughter.'

She was in a room decorated with a motive of flowers, more blooms, real, standing in vases their colors mixed in thick profusion. A swirl of changing light on a wall provided a focal point of interest and a window gave a view of the pines and snow-capped mountains.

A nice, clean, well-furnished room. One which belonged to a hotel or a guest house or an expensive asylum.

'Celia!' Feyman crossed to where she stood. 'Celia, girl! How are you?'

The bed was beside her providing a support for her knee and he guessed a nurse had placed her there as she had arranged for one hand to be resting on a small table placed on her opposite side. A stance which made her appear natural as did the embroidered robe he had given her, the rich fabric graced with a pattern of birds, fish and beasts. One he had been prompted to buy by some vague association between the life it portrayed and that he hoped to stimulate. A failure. The robe had done nothing but cover her body.

'Celia!' His hands gripped her arms. 'Answer me, girl! Answer me!'

'Steady.' Ganter was at his side. 'There's no point in shouting. No need to whisper, either. You know that. She can't hear you either way.'

21

A house deserted by its owner, left as an empty shell, indifferent and uncaring to whoever called. A girl, twenty years old, full of life and vitality, turned suddenly into something less than human.

A zombie.

Feyman swallowed and forced himself to be calm. No problem had ever been solved by hysterical ranting. Now, more than ever, Celia needed him. Alone she would die of thirst or starvation or a crippling fall. She was more helpless than a baby, more vulnerable than a newborn child.

He said, 'Somehow, somewhere, she must have picked up something. A germ of some kind. A virus.'

'Nothing shows in any of the tests.'

'A parasite of some kind?'

'If it's there we can't find it.'

'Poison? Nerve-gas?'

'The first thing we checked. A complete tox-scan was made of blood and bone. Negative. We probed deeper with the same result. All we discovered is what she'd eaten and drunk. The only drug residue was that of a compound used to neutralize the effects of alcohol.'

'A drug?'

'It was harmless. One of the sobup range.'

Feyman said, 'She wasn't alone. No harm in that but he could have primed her in some way. Fed her dope to boost her sexual appetite.'

'No.' Ganter was firm. 'We found no trace of anything like that.'

'Maybe you didn't check her in time?'

'She was taken ill in the Tycho Hilton. The resident physician was at her side within ten minutes of the incident. Like all such physicians he has an established procedure and made routine checks; drugs, dope, induced psycho-stimulation. Sex enhancers are among the first things they look for especially when dealing with the young. Her companion had taken a boost but she was clear. It's all in the report.'

Which he had read but words carried more information than print and he was sensitive to lies. Ganter wasn't lying — Celia had carried no destructive chemical or natural agent in her body

23

when found. If she had there would have been no problem. A cure or a funeral — and in the latter case the aftermath of a bloody revenge.

How had it happened?

Why?

Ganter said, 'I'm certain we can rule out any thought of infection or contamination. There have been no other cases from the Tycho Hilton and it seems she stayed close to the complex.'

'No other cases?' Feyman had caught the inflexion. 'From the Hilton, no, but from elsewhere? There are others?'

'Cases with similar symptoms? Yes. As we don't know the cause we can't be certain they are related. But they have one common factor — all are zombies.'

'How many?'

'The world-count is close to a hundred. Ninety-three to be precise but there could be others as yet unreported and, of those which have been not all need stem from the same cause.'

'You knew this and didn't tell me?'

'We discovered it,' corrected Ganter. 'Did you think we were doing nothing?

The data turned up when a scan was made of all similar cases but there hasn't been time as yet to make an in-depth investigation. It could be nothing but coincidence; zombie-like symptoms are not uncommon in many mental and physical illnesses. But we will do what we can.'

Given time and money — lots of money, but they could have all he owned if Celia could be cured. Feyman looked to where she had been placed. Her autonomic system had maintained her balance but soon it would fail. Already she was beginning to quiver a little, the hand resting on the table moving further from her side as the platform slid away.

Feyman reached her, caught her arms, urged her to turn. Obediently she obeyed. He saw her blink and felt a wild hope then remembered the action was an autonomic function. As the backs of her knees hit the edge of the bed he pushed a little, supporting her as she sat, the pressure of his hand preventing her from falling to lie on her back.

He said, 'These others — have any died?'

'Some.' Ganter was reluctant to talk about it. 'From internal bleeding, pneumonia, other infections. Many are in the remote areas and far from medical attention. Some had relatives who were careless.'

That and poor and unable to take care of an unwanted burden. Feyman looked at his child and tried to imagine himself as a peasant with debts to pay and no labor to spare and other mouths to feed. To such the death of the afflicted would be a mercy.

Celia sighed as he let her down to lie face-upwards on the bed. Air expelled from her lungs by a shift of external pressure but the sound made her suddenly human and young and Feyman blinked as his vision blurred and his eyes stung a little. Something that hadn't happened for a long time now.

'Those others died because they didn't receive proper care,' said Ganter. He couldn't read minds but it took no skill to read Feyman's expression. 'Celia won't get pneumonia or gangrene or any of a dozen infections. She won't starve and won't be left alone. Trust me.'

'I trust you.' Feyman rose and turned to look down at his daughter. 'But it's my girl, not yours. If she goes you've lost a patient. There'll always be more patients. I've only the one daughter.'

'I understand.'

Feyman doubted it. He looked at Celia seeing what the other man could never see for Ganter couldn't know. The hair, the line of the jaw, the cheeks, the set of the lips. Beauty now dust but which had once been close. The woman who had loved him and who had filled his life. Giving him the child that had grown into a woman in turn.

He said, 'Give me the truth, Ganter. Do you honestly claim you can cure her?'

'It's a matter of time. Tomorrow, a few weeks or months — who can tell?'

Words spoken by a salesman who was no longer smiling. A man of medicine but a salesman just the same and one following an old, familiar pattern. The spiel. The ritual followed because there was nothing better to offer the distressed. Hope served on a platter of euphemisms and what doctor could do otherwise? Ganter was only revealing his need to survive in the world he had made his own. When all else failed he had nothing left but to offer the need for faith.

'I'm taking Celia home,' said Feyman. 'Tomorrow morning. Arrangements will have to be made. See that she is ready.'

The nurses watched him go then returned to their charge. Ganter watched as they put Celia to bed then told them what had been decided. The eldest pursed her lips with disapproval.

'He cannot be rational. To take this poor child away — what does he hope to gain?'

'Gain?' Ganter shrugged. He had been through it before but still it left him bitter. There were more ways than one to fail. 'He wants more than I can deliver. More than anyone can deliver if they're honest. He wants a miracle and we don't keep them in stock.'

'Does anyone?'

'There are plenty who claim they do. Fakes, quacks, charlatans, phonies — Feyman's on a panic-run and has to try them all. *Has* to. If he doesn't he'll never be certain that the one he missed didn't have the answer.' Ganter paused then, with rare vehemence, added, 'The poor bastard. There's no way he can win.'

3

Taro Setuaka paused in his progress through the garden and delicately sniffed at a newly opened bloom. A gesture that displayed the finely modeled structure of his skull, the thin, aesthetic qualities of his face. One as ageless as stone, touched with a mesh of delicate lines, the eyes liquid, the nostrils arched and sensitive. He shivered a little as a breeze disturbed the flowers.

'It grows late, my friend. You will forgive me if I crave your indulgence. At this time of day I always take tea.'

As, at certain times of the day, he always did other things. A discipline Feyman could understand but not admire. A man was more than a machine to travel a regular journey from dawn to sunset. Something other than a prisoner of his own routines.

Politely he said, 'You have been most gracious. I am honored that you have granted me your hospitality. I had hoped to discuss a certain matter with you but, if the time is not right or you chose not to alter the direction of your mind, I understand.'

'Will you join me in tea?'

'I would be honored.'

'The courtesy of the guest enhances the pleasure of the host.' Setuaka bowed. 'I trust you will find it to your liking.'

It was dark bitter, served in the traditional manner. A ritual now mostly reserved for tourists who searched for mysteries in an ancient way of life not realizing that they, and so much more, had vanished when sun-bright atoms had signaled the event of a new era. But he had come too far and needed too much to argue if his host wanted to play games.

Dutifully Feyman sipped and tried to ignore the ache in calves and thighs. Close to fifty was no age to squat.

'You are comfortable?' Setuaka turned towards him, tiny cup in hand. 'Physical discomfort will detract from the enjoyment of the tea.'

'I can manage.'

'Which is to say that you lack true comfort but will not make an issue of it. Odd how words can have so many meanings. Have you knowledge of languages other than your own?'

'A smattering. I was in the Middle East for a while.'

'A restless area. You have been back there?'

'Recently.'

'Of course. The search for truth leads a man on a wending path. More tea? No? Then let us find you comfort in which to talk.'

Setuaka rose, satisfied at the service paid to tradition, becoming more alert as he led the way into his inner study. Here the floor was free of cushions and there were no low tables or lacquered bowls. A sophisticated computer terminal stood against one wall and Setuaka smiled as his guest glanced towards it.

'To admire the past is not to deride the future. Each age has something to give.'

'Old truths — new ways.'

'As you say. Now please be seated. You will find that chair more comfortable than the cushion you have just left. And please do not look so surprised. I live by ritual as you know but a certain time is set aside for such occasions as this. A time of non-discipline, you might say. A time of — panic? Is that the correct word? Panic?'

A time of non-discipline? Feyman said, 'Yes. I suppose some would call it that.'

'And others would call it the general survival syndrome. But what does the label matter if the object is the same? When all is lost then nothing can be lost. Some sit and resign themselves to the inevitable taking time, perhaps, to appreciate the beauty of a flower. Others will struggle until the end. I think you are one of them.' Setuka paused as if waiting for an answer then, when none came, said, 'Why have you come to me?'

'For help.'

'At least you are direct. Now prove to me that you have intelligence — why should I help you?'

A test? Feyman had heard about the mystic from others but no two stories were the same. Some had been given what they asked without question or hesitation, others denied, all had gained a different impression of the man. He seemed to live in a frugal manner but his robe was costly as was his abode. A guide. An advisor and counselor to the wealthy — some of their riches must have found their way into his account.

Feyman said, 'I can give you no good answer. You will help me if that is what you decide to do. There is no way I can make you. No way I can persuade you. I can only ask for you to do what you can.'

'Which could be nothing.'

'Which, by itself, proves you to be honest.'

The right reply? Feyman saw the lined face twitch in what could have been the dawning of a smile. One dying as Setuaka turned to touch flame to a stick of incense. As smoke threaded upwards the room became filled with the scent of oranges.

'A pleasant odor.' The mystic inhaled. As he released his breath he smiled and said. 'Talk to me, my friend. Tell me of what has gone before.'

The journeys to sacred places. The

shrines and caves and grottoes hung with discarded crutches and surgical appliances left by grateful suppliants. The healers who claimed too much and provided too little. The odd, disturbed mutants who had managers who battened on the credulity of their followers. The psychic surgeons who were simple illusionists and the hypnotists who were entertainers. The leaders of self-revealed faiths. The liars. The cheats. The frauds. The charlatans who waited like vultures to feed on the sick and frightened. Those to whom pity was measured in cash.

'What else did you expect?' Setuaka had sat like an idol until Feyman had come to the end. 'A miracle?'

'I was hoping to find one.'

'And are disappointed because you didn't. Have you spoken to Basro Shuftan?'

Feyman blinked at the sudden change of subject. 'I have.'

'And?'

'He couldn't help me but I respect the man for his honesty. He pointed out that I could be making a mistake in trying to find a cure for Celia.'

'Because she, in his opinion, need not be the victim of an ailment but something else?'

'Yes. He spoke of Nirvana and how people worked all their lives to gain one step towards it. Celia, he thought, could have possibly achieved it.'

'Nirvana,' mused Setuaka. 'The state where the soul is released from the bondage of flesh. The release from personal struggle and the end of personal existence. A hard concept for an occidental to accept. An almost impossible one to be considered desirable based, as your culture is, on personal achievement, personal wealth and status. As, no doubt, Basro Shuftan considered. His advice?'

'To do nothing. To accept.'

'Which you found lacking in comfort. And yet what better advice could he have given?'

Another test? The eyes of the Japanese were hard then he turned to pass his hand through the rising plume of incense, studying the writhing pattern he had

36

made. The scent of oranges turned to that of lavender.

Feyman said, 'To a man of his own culture, none. But I do not have the temperament that allows me to do nothing. And I find it hard to accept the unacceptable — no, I find it impossible. To do nothing. To accept.' His tone was bitter. 'If I'd been willing to do that Celia would still be in the clinic.'

And he'd still be working full time to enhance his fortune. If nothing else the search had given him the illusion of doing something useful. And yet had he been selfish? Was all this chasing about for Celia's sake or because he could not bear to be fronted with the accusation of apathy if she shouldn't make it? How much pain was caused by those claiming to act from unselfish motives?

'Too much, my friend,' murmured Setuaka. 'No, I cannot read your mind, but it isn't hard to guess what you are thinking. And your face betrays you. But you must not blame yourself for being what you are. Should a cat claw itself because it has no wings? A scorpion sting itself to death because it has no fins? A man should be what he is and not tear himself apart with futile longings.'

He lit another stick of incense.

'To return to your problem. Since you first contacted me I have done some research. The number of persons similarly affected to your daughter is in the region of a thousand. This is not a sudden increase in the number given you by Ganter but a revised estimate based on a review of delayed information from medical centers dealing with neurological diseases. In other words there have been far too many cases of wrong diagnosis. How many is too early to tell as yet but it could well be ten times as many.'

'Ten thousand!'

'A tiny proportion of the total population but one large enough to create a problem. The ailments that can affect a single individual have no real significance. They could be the result of gene damage or unsuccessful mutation. The human body and brain are highly complex assemblies and we know from our own efforts how complex apparatus is subject to unexpected perturbation.'

Feyman nodded, wondering at the reason for the lecture.

'As we get more sophisticated equipment the oddities in behavior tend to increase. The more elaborate the installation the greater the chance that each component will not function at all times as desired. So back-up systems are incorporated to ensure safety levels and the cost of continual maintenance is an important factor in every operation. The same pattern can be observed in societies. If we accept certain philosophies an individual is a sample of his culture. One that is in a state of expanding flux caused by the introduction of the zipships. But you know about those.'

'How — ?' Feyman shrugged, feeling stupid. The computer would have told Setuaka all he wanted to know about his visitor as it would tell him all he wanted to know about so much else. The modern oracle. 'Yes,' he admitted. 'I know about the zipships.'

He had introduced them. He had found the genius who had discovered the drive and had raised money for the initial company. A monopoly that hadn't lasted long — who could have clung to that pot of gold? But it had lasted long enough to lay the foundation of his fortune.

He said, 'Surely complexity alone cannot be the reason for the breakdowns? Why some and not others? Aren't we all complex too?'

'Perhaps.' Setuaka glanced towards a clock as it emitted a soft chime. 'Or perhaps we are more simple than we imagine. Much depends on the point of view. You are disappointed?'

'I had hoped for more.'

'Why? I am not a physician. I cannot work magic. I am unable to call on secret powers. I merely study what I see and one thing, to me, is obvious. It is that you have fallen into the trap of thinking that exotic cultures are more knowledgeable than your own. I find that strange. What have outmoded faiths to do with you? Obsolete beliefs and tattered superstitions? Have you ever believed in rain gods? Ghosts? Wood demons? The efficiency of spells? And if you do not believe in them how can you have any real contact with those who do?'

'Are you saying such beliefs are false?'

'Not to those immersed in them. An individual is a sample of the culture that shaped him. Into which would you fit?'

Not into one which sipped bitter tea and squatted on cushions. The chair had been a welcome relief and, suddenly, Feyman realized the ceremony had been more than what it seemed. A lesson without words; the obvious made clear by analogy — almost he had missed it.

'A mirror,' he said abruptly. 'Is that how you work? Helping people by showing them just what they are?'

'Usually it is sufficient.'

'And if it isn't?'

'The cat will continue to claw at itself because it isn't a bird. The scorpion to sting because it isn't a fish. You know that. You are too old not to have learned it. Too wealthy not to have found the way to survive in your own culture.' Setuaka passed his hand through the smoke of the incense. 'What more can I say?'

He had illustrated a point and reminded

Feyman of his youth, the early days of struggle, the stroke of fortune that had made him rich. But the money had not come easily and if he had done nothing, accepted the first refusal, the chance would have been lost. A fighter. He looked at his hands, the faded scars on his knuckles, the jagged cicatrice on his left wrist. Once he had known how to fight. Really fight, not with paper and cash and whispers to politicians in the shadows but man to man, slugging it out, tasting blood and knowing hurt.

He was still a fighter — why had he scoured the world searching for a miracle?

'Panic,' said Setuaka when, bluntly, he asked the question. 'A temporary madness. Yet it was something you had to do.'

'I still have to do it but I chose the wrong way. You've shown me that.'

Setuaka bowed, the clock chiming its softly dominating note as he straightened. As it faded he said, 'It is time for you to leave now. Soon I must be alone to meditate. I shall not see you again but, my friend, there is no need. You know what you must do.'

'Stick to my own.' Feyman squared his shoulders conscious of a new strength, a revived determination. 'Work within familiar parameters.'

'Exactly.'

Setuaka bowed again, an ancient gesture born in a time of rigid deference. A part of an alien culture as was the tea, the cushion, the incense, the elaborate courtesy. One of which Feyman had no part. Politeness dictated that he leave without another word. Need made him linger.

'Please.' He took a step towards the Japanese. 'Help me just a little more. It will save time if nothing else and I've wasted enough of that already. Even to work in my own culture I need help. Who is best suited to give it?'

For a moment he thought the request would be ignored then, as the clock chimed for the third time, Setuaka said, 'There are many who would be willing but one I can recommend. Lynne Colman. The last time we were in contact she lived in Pasadena.'

4

Pasadena was like an old woman who had put away the delights of passion and had found a serenity in the calm observance of external stupidity. Secluded buildings ringed the city; complexes with resident guards, others set within wide lawns, a few built like castles, most containing the elements of medieval strongholds. Feyman had bought one, staffing it with a doctor, nurses, others necessary to his plan.

He hadn't anticipated a siege.

They blocked the car as it swung into the drive; a motley collection of tattered robes, bizarre hats, beards, bare feet, beads. The children of the children of those who had looked for paradise in a flower.

'What the hell's going on?'

The driver shrugged. 'They've come down from Los Angeles mostly but we have our own brand of kook. They're making a brace.'

'What?'

'They've learned who you are and why you're here.' The driver, a local, was patient. 'Some newshound gained the story and spread it around. You're news, Mister Feyman, and you're rich. You've also got a problem and those zanies want to solve it for you. They'll hang around until you do something.'

'Such as?'

'As I said, it's a brace. They want a handout. You could give them a few hundred and accept their blessing and they'd go.'

'And tomorrow?'

'They'll be back or others like them.' The driver added, after a moment, 'Of course you could hire a corps of security guards with dogs and guns and the rest of it. Or call the police or just blast them with hoses but there's an easier way. Just pick the strongest bunch and hire them to do the job.'

'I won't have scum like that in the house.'

'They'll stay outside. Just pay them and let them chant and pray. If anything good happens they'll claim the credit. If not you get blamed for not letting them get close. Either way you get peace. Want me to arrange it?'

All it took was money. The leader of the selected group, a giant negro with spiked hair, scarred cheeks and a magnificent body cleared the area and set up five altars at equal points to form a pentagram, A disciple at each, two acolytes to aid each disciple and three attendants at each station to keep the incense burning and to keep up the chanting provided enough manpower to ensure privacy.

From where he stood in an upper room of the house Doctor Sam Wolfe said, 'Well, it works. That particular kind of magic, I mean. Muscle backed by money — an irresistible combination.'

He was young, inclined to flip humor, but good at his job. Feyman had picked him and Wolfe was fully aware the position would either make him rich or dead. He and four nurses took care of Celia. Two of them, at least, Feyman was certain had shared his bed. Not that it mattered. Not unless his lust reduced his efficiency.

As he turned from the window Feyman said, 'News?'

'Nothing. Celia's condition is unchanged. You?'

Feyman shook his head. He'd been to a village in the hinterland of Mexico. A doctor, dying of disease and peyote, had shown him a woman, old, seamed, sitting like a vegetable on a heap of filthy rags. A zombie. One covered with sores, the flies thick around her eyes.

He said, 'This woman was working in the fields some months ago. A hard-working, devout woman. A good wife and mother. When she did not return home to prepare the evening meal they looked for her. They found her like this.'

'Had she been ill?'

'No.'

'What does her family think is wrong?'

'She now has no family. They think she is cursed and have abandoned her.' The doctor lifted a gourd to his mouth. Lowering it he spoke with even more careful deliberation than before. 'She is dying. She will die. Nothing can be done. When dead she will be burned and her ashes buried. Mass will be said for the repose of her soul. Nothing more can be done.'

A woman already considered dead. Left, abandoned, ignored. Feyman had pushed money into her lax hand, knowing it would be taken but hoping the taker would be charitable. It would have been more merciful to have put a bullet through her heart.

Wolfe said, 'It was a wild chase. I thought you'd got over that.'

He had but the journey had filled time and he was too restless to sit and do nothing. In the office his secretary looked up from his desk. Frank Harman was older than Feyman, thinner, his manner that of a man who had found refuge in anonymity.

'Some messages, sir. Aston from New York wants to know your decision as regards the Nitackie-Haite merger. Sturn from Zurich has a question as to your holding in the Mohen Consortium. An offer for you to buy option-shares has been received from the Quaker-Vire Trust — a returned favor as I understand it. Salem Bey in — '

'Any word from Lynne Colman?'

'As yet, sir, no.'

'Damn!'

Lynne Colman was hard to find. Her house in Pasadena had been let on a long-term lease to a family from Ontario; one room retained for personal use if and when she ever decided to return. The latest information placed her in the Belt, on Ceres where she worked for some combine. Feyman wasn't sure which but had circulated them all. As yet she hadn't bothered to reply.

'Get me Brennan.' It was time to use more than patience. As the screen cleared to show a seamed and lined face Feyman said, 'Sorry to wake you, Jack. This is urgent.'

'What isn't?'

'Lynne Colman. She works with computers and is somewhere in the Belt. On Ceres, I think,'

'So?'

'I want her.'

'To work for you?' Brennan shrugged. His eyes were puffed and his hair a mess. A man ten thousand miles away in a different time zone. 'Why don't you just ask her?'

'I've tried. She doesn't seem interested. I've heard nothing from her.'

'So you've got your answer.'

'One I don't like. Fix it, Jack. Do it fast.'

'I'll do what I can. Give me time.' The screen went blank and Feyman stretched. To Harman he said, 'Let me know when he calls. Wake me if you have to.'

'Yes, sir. These other matters?'

Details Feyman took care of with trained precision. Once such financial manipulations had held a rich satisfaction but now the shifting of capital, the buying and selling of stock held a dry emptiness. Celia had done that; her illness reminding him of the true meaning of life. His travels too — exotic philosophies had rubbed off on his previous assurance. But in his culture money was power and without it a man was nothing.

'Tell Weeman to sell when the Oldupt Mines reach the figure I sent him. Sheem will be in contact to arrange an exchange. Stall him.' Feyman looked at the desk, 'Is that all? Good. Update the record.'

To wait for Brennan's call was a torment he could do without. He felt hot, sticky and a shower seemed in order. He heard the scream as he left the office and was halfway up the stairs before the echoes died.

He was fast but Minchin was faster, the bodyguard at the door of the room next to Celia's before Feyman had reached the landing. It crashed open, a nurse shouting from within; Avril Kinski who had screamed. A brown figure wearing a turban and a white robe writhed in Minchin's big hands.

'Hold it!' Feyman's call halted the fist that would have slammed the stranger unconscious. To the brown man he said, 'What's this all about? Who are you? How did you get into the house?'

'My name is Ahmed Ranjha and to me no door is barred. I pass through walls as I pass through mountains with the aid of the powers granted to me by the mighty Brahma, the Lord of Creation.' The turbaned head bowed. 'I came to help you. As proof of my forbearance I will not destroy the one who laid violent hands on my person.'

'A nut.' Wolfe had joined the assembly. 'Shall I take care of him?'

'Celia?'

'I've just checked her. She's fine. He never got close to her.'

'He was in a wardrobe,' said Avril Kinski. 'He jumped out at me.' More scared than she had been and she felt foolish at having screamed. 'Why not just throw him out?'

'First we find out how he got in here.' Feyman nodded at Minchin who closed his hand on the intruder's thin shoulder. 'Well?'

'I told you — '

'Lies. I want the truth. Unless I get it the man holding you will break every bone in your body.' Feyman thrust his face forward, the eyes hard, the mouth cruel. A signal and Ranjha screamed as the bodyguard tightened his grip. The pressure eased as Feyman lifted a hand. 'Start talking.'

'I came early yesterday in a cabinet holding machinery. At night I hid in that room. I was waiting.' He straightened as Minchin removed his hand. 'I came to help,' he said with forced dignity. 'To save your daughter from the curse which has been placed on her.'

A curse — Feyman remembered the woman in Mexico, the way she had sat, her sores, the flies, the indifference of those who should have loved her. Could curses hold power?

'You think she has been cursed?'

'That is my opinion. I must examine her to be sure.'

'Can you cure her?'

'With the aid of Brahma all things are possible. May I confirm my opinion?'

Feyman watched as Wolfe led the man into Celia's room. Minchin, eager to redeem his failure at having allowed an intruder to get so close, watched like a hawk as Ranjha chanted and knelt before the girl. Lifting his hands he held them before her eyes, palms facing her, the skin

53

traced with red and yellow designs. As he moved them slowly from side to side a thin, droning wail keened from his lips.

'Fascinating.' Wolfe glanced at Feyman. 'The initial steps to achieving a hypnotic trance. With a suggestible person it would work every time.'

'You don't like it?'

'It isn't medicine.'

'Which makes it — what?' Feyman watched the man kneeling before the girl. Ranjha was now swaying, his entire body keeping time to the rhythmic movements of his hands. 'Magic? Superstition? Give it a name.'

'Charlatanism.'

'And if it works?'

It wouldn't and Feyman knew it. He had seen men like Ranjha before, heard equal conviction, listened to equal promises. Always there had been failure. He wasn't surprised when the man ceased to sway and drone, leaning forward to peer into the vacuous blue eyes. He even knew what Ranjha would say.

'A most difficult case. Even with my powers it will not be easy to remove the curse that afflicts her but it can be done. This I promise.'

'When?'

'How long will it take?' Ranjha pursed his lips. 'A few days. At the most a week. With the right assistance I could do it within a few hours. It will not be easy but I promise it will be done. With your help, of course. I cannot do it alone.'

Feyman said, dryly, 'Help?'

'There are essential items needful to the ceremony; spices to be burned, holy patterns of great power to be assembled, sacred vessels and esoteric devices. The beneficial energies of kindly powers must be united and directed with the use of traditional offerings. As an analogy think of the use of platinum as a catalyst. A ruby to provide a lasering effect. The forces I handle, while less crude, hold vast potential. With their aid I will venture into the Dark Regions to summon the spirit of your daughter. I shall remove the curse that has blighted her. I will guide her back and make all well. This I promise.'

'If I give my help?'

'Yes.'

Feyman said, with sudden impatience, 'You're talking about money. How much?'

'Does a surgeon name a sum when he asks for a scalpel? A physician when he needs to use a special drug?'

'Quit the crap! How much?'

'You talk of reward? Of expense? I have asked for nothing. If you have your daughter well again you must trust me. Who else knows better than myself what I need? Who can better anticipate the trend of psychic events? Already I see her, smiling, reaching out her hands towards you. For me that, in itself, would be reward enough. But how is a man to pluck the fruit without a ladder to climb the tree?'

Feyman looked at his hands and forced himself to be calm. Another con. Another scrap of human filth homing in like a vulture to offer hope as a bribe and who knew nothing of pity.

Ranjha mistook his silence. 'Sir, if you will trust me. An open draft to obtain the necessary items. Limit it as you will — I will do the best with what you can afford.'

Feyman said, 'I'll tell you what — cure her and I'll give you ten million dollars. Take your time about it. Get everything you need and let me have the bills. But, if you fail I'll have my people fix things so that you spend a month dying. That's one promise you can believe.'

'You are against me.' Ranjha swallowed, suddenly afraid. 'All of you are against me. I sense your hostility. I cannot remain in an atmosphere of such hate.'

'You promised,' said Feyman. 'You tried to give me hope.'

'I — '

'You're a liar of the worst kind. Scum! Filth! A disease!' Feyman looked at Minchin. 'Get him out of here.'

Ranjha squealed as he was lifted off his feet and run down the stair to the door. As the panel swung open the bodyguard yelled, 'Hey! You out there! Look what sneaked in past you! If it happens again we'll buy new magic! Catch?'

The man and the message both. Feyman heard the yells and whoops, the screams, the sound of blows as the intruder was given painful memories to take on his way. An empty revenge and one that brought no satisfaction.

Back in his office he said, 'Any word yet from Brennan?'

'No, sir.' Harman pursed his lips. 'I'll call you when he does.'

A delicate reminder that Brennan didn't like to be chased. That to call again to hurry things along would be a mistake. That all Feyman could do now was to wait.

5

A storm building in the Pacific had been dispersed by the Weather Corps; zipship implosions breaking up the accumulation and sending streamers of cloud in a scattered dispersal-pattern over the coast. The rain had washed the air and streets and Feyman wished it had washed away his own problems at the same time.

Three days now and still no word from Brennan or Lynne Colman. The zanies had gone replaced by more orthodox guards and he could have lived in protected isolation. Instead he had chosen to entertain visitors.

So the priests had come bearing the instruments of exorcism, and the Holy Women with their prayers, the faith healers and the expert from Haiti who had stared into Celia's empty eyes and departed muttering of Voodoo. Now he listened to the frighteningly calm voice of a man who had to be insane.

'My master says you have no need to fear. The condition of your daughter is merely a manifestation of the Supreme Universality and has been predetermined from the beginning of time. The human race is bound for a destiny shaped by those who first fashioned the design of flesh and bone that makes it what it is. In ages past they came in vehicles from a distant place to manipulate the germ plasm and establish the DNA pattern and so set their stamp on what we are. He says she is the one who goes before the man riding the white horse who will be bearing a single flower. I am not sure exactly what that means but the message is clear.'

One relayed, if Paul Seeton could be believed, from an incredibly ancient, god-like alien who lived in a vast cavern deep beneath the turbulent surface of the planet Venus. An overseer of a kind, set to watch over the progress and development of the mutated creatures that had become Mankind.

Feyman said, 'Can you cure my daughter?'

'I can do nothing. I am merely the tool used by my master to communicate his desires. Think of me as a transceiver — you talk and my master hears. He communicates and my mouth gives utterance to his thoughts.'

Glib, but everything about the man was that as all about his appearance inspired confidence. No robes, no beard, bare feet, lank hair, painted cheeks. He looked a successful businessman; middle-aged, neat, calm, placid, educated as his genuine degrees proved. Even his name held a comforting ordinariness.

'How did it happen?' said Feyman. 'How did you become as you are?'

'It just happened.' Seeton answered the question as he must have done a thousand times before. 'One evening I fell asleep while watching television and, in my sleep, I was transported from my corporeal body to the great cavern of my master and there instructed as to what I was to be. Always there has been such as I to act as the emissaries of the Ancient Power. In times past we have been used to determine the course of events such as when — ' Seeton broke off, his eyes rolling upward, head tilted as if he listened to a distant voice. 'Yes, master,' he murmured. 'It shall be as you order.' To Feyman he said, 'My master does not wish to divulge more at this time but he will answer any questions you may care to ask.'

'How long has he been residing on Venus?'

'My master gives a figure of twenty-three elgash which translates into something close to three hundred and eighty thousand years. However he points out that time is a variable equation when considered in the terms imposed by the secondary field of haladashen forces.'

'What must I do to cure Celia?'

'My master assures you that your daughter is not ill. Her ego-awareness has simply been transported to another plane and another dimension in order that she should gain harmony with the great pool of intelligences that is the supreme Universality. My master suggests you think of it as an ocean filled with an infinite number of drops. Each drop

forms an individual awareness. No — '
Again Seeton broke off to lift his eyes
upward and to appear to listen.

'I am at fault. My master points out
that my analogy was not a good one. He
would rather you think of a cavern filled
with all forms of life. The awareness
of each creature is revealed as a glow of
light. That belonging to low forms will be
small; an insect would barely be visible, a
cat more so, a dog brighter still, a human
the brightest of all. But some humans will
shine brighter than others because within
them is more of the Supreme Universality. My master wishes to know if you
understand.'

Feyman nodded. A life-force dished out
in varying amounts; the greater the
portion the greater the intelligence.

'What happens when someone dies?'

'There is no death, no cessation. When
an organism ceases to function the
individual awareness returns to the
Supreme Universality. It becomes again a
part of the whole. The concept of death
and of loss as you know it is without
meaning. As my master says; does the

ocean mourn the spilling of a wave? Hate the presence of a cloud? When all is one then one must be all.' Seeton gave a depreciating smile. 'My master assures me you are able to grasp the concept but it is one which has nuances which elude me. In any case my master asks that you retain an open mind. By doing so you will find comfort.'

If so it had yet to come and his patience was getting short. Feyman snapped, 'You came offering to help.'

'My master directed me to come to you,' corrected Seeton. 'He tells me your destiny is linked closely to the path chosen for humanity to take. That in you resides much — ' he frowned. 'Much — ' A shrug and another depreciating smile. 'I am sorry but I really cannot translate the concept which my master wishes to convey. A near approximation would be godliness — no, not that. Power? Greatness? My master tells me the word will serve. You are possessed of much greatness.' He paused, listening, then with an abrupt change of subject, 'My master wishes you to test a certain matter. Please give me your hand.'

In it he placed a small, round instrument. A thermometer graded in the Celsius scale. The red-tipped pointer hovered at 37 — normal body temperature. Feyman looked at it. A test? Some kook trickery?

'My master asks that you watch the instrument,' directed Seeton. 'He will give a small demonstration of your abilities. You will continue to feel comfortable. You will not experience any pain. My master asks that you watch the thermometer. Watch the hand. Watch as it moves.

To 39 . . . 47 . . . 69 . . . 85 . . . 98 . . . 106 . . . 123 . . . 174 . . . At 200 it halted.

'Water boils at one hundred degrees Celsius,' pointed out Seeton. 'My master reminds you that your temperature is now twice that of boiling water as you can see. Yet he assures me that you feel no discomfort and will experience no harm.' A pause then, 'My master will terminate the demonstration. When your temperature returns to normal he asks that you hand the instrument to me.'

Feyman flung the instrument towards the other man not looking at the pointer. 'What do you want from me?'

Smiling, Seeton said, 'My master senses that you do not fully understand, He wishes to give not to receive. He tells me that I should leave you now. Before I go I am instructed to give you a thought on which to ponder. It is this; if you take two items and place them together what, exactly, do you have?'

Alone Feyman roved the house. To sit with Celia would achieve nothing and aside from disturbing the routine of her care would create within himself a corroding depression. The office was empty; Harman having left for the East to tie up a business deal. Feyman should have gone in person but other things held greater importance. Brennan, Colman — where the hell was the woman?

His shoes made hard rapping noises as he descended the stairs to the basement. Lights made it brighter than day and some men were busy clearing up a heap of broken crates and discarded cartons. In a chamber to one side Tony Drummer was making some final checks.

'Hi!' He lowered his clipboard as Feyman joined him. 'Come to look at the new baby?'

He was young, brash, brimming with confidence. He'd made a killing and he knew it. The deal with Feyman would make him top salesman of the year and open the way to a desk in the executive chamber of the firm he represented.

'The finest hardware money can buy!' He gestured at the computer terminal set against the far wall. 'That thing's damned near alive. You've done well, sir, my word on it.'

His and the other experts Feyman had consulted and Drummer would never know he'd been given the business to sweeten someone in his firm. He'd get the credit but the cash would go where it counted.

'Has it been checked? Tested?'

'Three preliminary programs together with the usual cross-checks and balances. No bugs. No delays. No foul-ups. When Brico Electric deliver they provide nothing but the best.' Drummer turned as one of the workmen called to him. 'A moment.' He looked at Feyman. 'You want all the packing removed?'

'Yes.'

'If you want to shift this stuff it might be an idea to keep some by. No?' Drummer shrugged. 'A clean sweep,' he yelled. 'It all goes.'

The men went and the salesman leaving Feyman alone with the new installation. He crossed to it, touched it, letting his fingers trail over its smooth sleekness. A machine that could only be as good as the one using it. One that, maybe, would give him the answer and put the life back in Celia's eyes.

A computer and a skilled operator. Put two things together and what did you get?

The question nagged at him, as he returned upstairs. Seeton was a nut, he had to be, but was it fair to judge him from a biased standpoint? Others had claimed to hear voices and had ended as Prophets and Saints. Basically it was a matter of philosophy.

And that was at the heart of it, thought Feyman as he entered the room he used as a study. Just which philosophy was the best? To accept the dictates of fate as a Muslim would suggest? To bow to the will of God as a Christian or a Jew? To acknowledge the mysterious power of superior beings as did other religions? Was there none that told a man to stand up and fight? To spit in the eye of superstition?

Did Seeton have the right of it? Was there some ancient alien hiding somewhere and watching the development of an eon-old experiment? Was Mankind nothing more than that?

Fruit flies in a jar.

Creatures distorted by the curiosity of some alien scientist who hoped to achieve God alone knew what. One mirrored by those he had produced. Did men have to cripple living things in his search for knowledge? The clipped ears of dogs, the seared tissue, the docked tails, the inbreeding to create freaks. The mice given cancer, the rats sent mad, the kittens blinded, the rabbits, the newts and toads and moths and insects to which had been done unforgivable horrors. If these were creations of God why had he allowed them to be so abused?

Why Celia?

Brandy stood on the desk and the decanter chimed against the glass as he poured. Liquid gold that should have provided comfort but did little aside from stinging his throat. Setting down the glass he looked at it beside the decanter.

Two items, Seeton had said. Place them together and what did you have? No, what *exactly* did you have? The qualification made a difference.

A puzzle, then, one which reminded him of another given him by a Zen Buddhist — what is the sound of one hand clapping? A question that could not be answered and was not intended to be answered but was a device to stimulate the direction of thought.

Had Seeton or his master meant something on the same lines? Had it been a trick or empty mouthings?

Two items and what, exactly, did you have?

Two items, of course, but wait — suppose they were sugar and water mixed to form a syrup? Would you have two items or one? Was a compound a whole or the sum of its parts? But if the items were solid, the glass, for example, and the decanter. Two individual items which, if placed together, would form a set. Like a knife and fork, a bowl and spoon, a brush and comb. Two items or one? Or even three? The sum of both plus the thing they made when together?

What exactly did you have?

Wolfe entered the room while Feyman was still brooding on the problem. He said, 'Anything?'

'No.' Feyman glanced at the doctor. 'Am I such a fool?'

'I don't take you for one.'

'Some do.'

'Those that don't understand, maybe. To hell with them.' Wolfe dismissed the subject. 'I'd like to try a more intensive regimen of exercise. I want Celia to do more walking and other routine exercises, I'd also like her to swim.' He added, as Feyman frowned, 'She used to be quite proficient and her autonomic system will have retained the instilled reflexes. Also it is a basic function of the body to react to immersion in fluids.'

'Will it help?'

'Of course. It's important to maintain her muscle-tone. It may do no more than that but, when she recovers, she won't want to find herself wasted.'

When, not if. Feyman was grateful for that.

'One other thing,' said Wolfe. 'Ganter called. He said he was concerned with Celia's progress but his real reason was to find out if we'd stumbled on a cure or any chance of finding one. We fenced around quite a while then he decided to be honest. He's got another patient. The son of Jefek Furneaux. You probably know him.'

'We've met. His son, you say?'

'Saeed Furneaux, that's right. He was traveling in his private ship when — ' Wolfe snapped his fingers. 'He went zombie.'

'Just like that? Are you certain?'

'Ganter swore to it. There were a dozen witnesses. One second he was normal, laughing, joking. The next he was gone.'

'Where did it happen? Close to the Moon?'

'No. He was near the Belt. Heading for the Chang-Kei Cluster. The captain brought the ship back to Mars as soon as he knew there was trouble. He's been with Ganter three days now. He hinted he'd like Celia to return to the clinic.'

So as to bolster his reputation. Furneaux wouldn't leave his son long in the care of an advertised failure. Place two zombies together and you had more than a pair, you had an institution.

One that would pay well.

The phone called as Wolfe left the room. It was Brennan and his message was short.

Lynne Colman was on her way.

6

She was slim, richly brown, with short, dark hair and deep-set eyes. Cosmetics enhanced their luster as it did the soft fullness of her mouth. The figure beneath the pelted gown was smoothly feminine. A woman who could have been a model. One scant inches shorter than himself and close to twenty years younger. Feyman watched as she came towards him, held out his hand as she approached.

'Lynne Colman? This is a pleasure. I'm Max Feyman.'

She smiled as their fingers touched and assessed him in turn. Tall, well-preserved, no paunch and no sagging jowls. His eyes were blue, his hair brown, grizzled at the temples. His hands were broad, his grip firm.

A smooth façade; one she knew masked a hard and ruthless man.

'I've a car waiting.' he said. 'Have you luggage?'

'Stored. It can wait.'

'Shall we go?'

'We need to talk.'

'Of course. But not here.'

As usual the port was thronged, the air a vibrating discomfort from calls, greetings, shouts, the drone of voices from the public address system, the blur of zipnoise as ships arrived and left.

'Noise.' Lynne shook her head. 'I'd forgotten what it was like. This is a madhouse.'

One locked out as they settled in the rear compartment of the car. The driver sent it gliding from a group of sundancers as they moved to block the road. Before they could start performing police moved in with sprays that sent them retching to one side. One waved for the car to continue, saluting as it passed.

'Service,' said Lynne. 'With money you get it.'

Feyman ignored the remark. 'Did you have a pleasant journey?'

'It was fine as such things go.' Shades cut the sun glare and filled the interior of the limousine with a cool dimness. In it her teeth shone with startling clarity as she smiled. 'I've a message for you. Taro Setuaka sends his regards.'

'You've seen him? Is he well?'

'I spoke with him. As for the rest — ' She shook her head. 'He's dying.'

'I didn't know.'

'Why should you? That's why he lives the way he does. Each second must be made to yield its full potential. Each hour given to a different aspect of study. The world will be a poorer place when he has gone.'

Feyman nodded then, softly, quoted, 'If you can fill each and every minute with sixty seconds worth of distance run.'

'Kipling!' She radiated her pleasure. 'You've read him too. The end?'

Together they chanted its ending, ' — you will be a man, my son.'

'A man,' she mused. 'Just what is a man?'

'You too?' Feyman lifted his hands. 'Everyone I meet seems to be asking me questions. What is the sound of one hand clapping? What, exactly, are two things when placed together? What is a man?'

'Zen Buddism,' she said. 'The Arethians. Myself.'

'Arethians?'

'The new breed of those who claim they are in contact with an alien living in a cavern in Venus. They've been around almost a hundred years. They could even be right — as yet no one has managed to prove them wrong. Did you find the answers?'

'I'm not sure. One hand clapping is, I assume, a guide to study alternate frames of reference. The other that things are not always as they seem.' He told her of Seeton and the incident with the thermometer. 'It was gimmicked, of course. Set with a predetermined cycle activated by pressure before he put it into my hand. A trick.'

'Or maybe a demonstration to prove something,' she said. 'Things aren't always what they seem. But, if they aren't, then what are they?'

'I wouldn't know. I'm not a philosopher.'

'No,' she said. 'Maybe you aren't. But I'll tell you one thing, Max Feyman — I suspect you're a first-class bastard.'

He said nothing waiting, listening to the soft hum of the car as surging electrons sent it on its way.

She said, 'Did you hear me?'

'Would you rather I hadn't?'

'No — and don't take what I said as a compliment. I'm not one of those people who like to get kicked around.' She joined him in waiting then said, 'You haven't slapped me and you haven't halted the car to throw me out. I thought you'd do both. Taro warned me you are a dangerous man.'

'Did he tell you I'm also a desperate one?'

'Yes,' she admitted. 'I can believe it — there has to be some reason for you to arrange what you did. It couldn't have been cheap. Or do you deny you manipulated things on the Belt?' She waited then, when he made no answer, 'You don't admit it or deny it. Most men would like to boast — but most men are like small boys who just have to tell everyone just how clever and strong they are. The trouble with men like that is they forget others have a few brains too.'

'Especially when they're computer operators?'

'Technicians,' she corrected. 'Engineers. Harmonizers. Scheme-creators. Anyone can operate a computer. All you need do is press buttons.'

To find answers — what had she learned?

'Max Feyman,' she said. 'Forty-nine years old. One living child, Celia aged twenty. Her mother, your wife Blanche Svenguard, died sixteen years ago. Your first wife Shamarre and your son Michael died together in an accident five years before Celia was born. Your parents — ' She broke off then said, 'Do you want me to go on?'

'They died when I was a child,' he said. 'A lot of people died then at that time and at that place. I was lucky. A couple adopted me.' He added, bitterly, 'Some advice, Lynne Colman. When you put in the knife don't be afraid to turn it. That way the blood comes fast.'

'Don't talk to me about blood!' She radiated her anger. 'I was under contract to the Ling-Heywood Foundation based on Ceres. Nothing special but the work was interesting and I was set for the next three years. Which is why I didn't return your calls — there was no point. Maybe I should have been more polite, but — ' Her gesture was expressive. 'Things are different in the Belt.'

'So?'

'There was an accident. Nothing too serious but the computer facility I was using went dead. Suddenly I was surplus to requirement. That's a nice way of saying I no longer had a job. A mutual-canceling contract,' she explained. 'In the case of non-ability to carry out agreed duties either side has the right to terminate the agreement. Such contracts are common in the Belt. I found another facility and could have continued but there was some unexpected opposition.' She inhaled, nostrils flaring, the fabric of her gown taut over the mounds of her breasts. 'I found I had become very unpopular. The facility I'd found was withdrawn. I lost my living quarters and had to take others at double the cost.

People I thought were friends stopped being that. So I did a little digging and put things together and, well, here I am.'

'To work for me.'

'No. To tell you just where to shove your offer!' Anger twisted her face into the mask of a savage. 'Now tell your flunkey to halt this car and let me out!'

Feyman looked at her, doing nothing, counting the seconds. Her patience broke at twelve.

'Damn you! Stop this car!'

'It's a long walk back to town.

'You — '

'Shut up!' His hand lifted as if to slap her face. 'You've had your say and now it's my turn. So you zipped all the way from the Belt to tell me to go to hell. All right, you've done it, now act like the adult you're supposed to be. Have you proof that I got you fired?'

It couldn't exist, Brennan would have been too careful, but she had come uncomfortably close.

'No?' He lowered his hand as she shook her head. 'Proof that I had anything to do with anything else? Be honest, now.

Forget suspicions, I'm talking about proof.'

'You're talking about evidence,' she snapped. 'The red hand, the knife, the blood, the body. But people like you are too smart to leave that kind of proof lying around. I'm talking about coincidence and association. Why do you want me to work for you?'

'Setuaka recommended you.'

'And?'

'I made some enquiries. According to those who know about these things you're one of the best.'

'Not just one of them,' she corrected. 'I am the best. But you haven't answered my question — why do you want me to work for you?'

'I want you to save my daughter.'

She sat in a room bright with colored paintings; animals, clowns, rotund creatures, bizarre depictions of fairy-tale worlds. The harsh sunlight was softened by drapes but even so the light was bright enough to throw glints of silver from her hair. Standing before her Feyman moved a hand before her eyes, expecting the non-reaction but wishing they had followed the movement of his fingers. The lids remained wide even when he stabbed the tips towards them.

'You see?'

Lynne Colman nodded, looking at the girl. A body, one controlled by the 'primitive brain', the basic survival mechanism that did little more than ensure maintained existence. Lift her arm and it would remain extended until the autonomic nervous system decided it was time to rest the overstrained muscle and sinew. The system that kept her heart beating, her lungs at work, the sweat glands operating, her eyes moistened. Which kept her moving when asleep. Which emptied her bladder and bowels when they were full.

Things Feyman had explained before he had guided her into the room.

To the attendant nurse he said, 'Have you been reading to her as I ordered?'

'Yes, sir.'

'I didn't hear your voice when I arrived.'

'I — ' She swallowed, conscious of

guilt. 'I must have paused for a few moments. Reading aloud hurts my throat after a while.'

He said nothing but examined the book. It was a picture book as he'd anticipated. Opening it he looked at the small screen, the figures moving in three-dimensional life. An earphone could be plugged in to listen to the narrator but otherwise words streamed up and over the screen. The text was the streamlined condensation of the author's original work, the pictures the artist's contribution, the whole a product of miniaturized technology. The book was Stevenson's *Treasure Island*.

'Good, isn't it?' The nurse was enthusiastic. 'It really moves.'

'Change it for something else. An old fashioned book.'

'Sir?'

'I want you to read to Celia and I mean read. Words spoken aloud. While watching this you tend to forget.'

He added, catching her expression, 'I realize it can be boring but it's part of the job. Do it or quit.'

As they left the room Lynne said, 'Can it help? The reading, I mean. Surely she must be deaf.'

'No, sounds register even if she doesn't respond. There's a system of therapy that claims that continual stimulus can promote a rapid development of mental faculties. It's based on visual effects, noise, tactile impressions; anything to capture and hold the attention. Wolfe designed the technique.'

'Her doctor?' As Feyman nodded she said, 'You were hard on that nurse. Do you like kicking people around?'

'No, but while they take my money they earn it.'

'As I'd have to do?'

'If you work for me — yes.'

'And you want that, don't you.' She took a deep breath. 'Want it a lot. Want it so much that you made damned sure I'd have no choice. Right?'

Feyman halted and turned to look down at her face, his eyes hard as they met her own.

He said, deliberately, 'You always have a choice. Everyone does. You can accept

85

my offer or tell me to shove it and walk out of here and go where the hell you please. But, if you do that, remember what you'll be leaving behind. Not just Celia but all the others like her. Thousands of them as far as I know. More — the number is growing all the time. You could help them.'

'How? I'm no doctor.'

'Doctors are helpless. They don't know what's wrong. They don't know what triggers the condition or how to cure it. Maybe, if they knew the cause, they could find the answer. I'm betting you can find the cause.'

'You want a miracle. I'm — '

'I know what you are.' Feyman was curt in his interruption. 'You have the brain and skill to wed yourself to a machine. To sort out ten billion facts and assemble enough of them to make a pattern which makes sense. You know the problem; zombies are popping up all over. How would you begin?'

'I'd need full details on each and every case; sex, age, educational accomplishment, physical make-up, time, position both geographical and social, clothing worn at the critical moment, food eaten, medication taken — ' She broke off, shrugging. 'Maybe a couple of hundred items for each case and that's only the beginning.'

'But you can do it.' Feyman turned away from her, took five long strides, returned to where she stood. 'Help me — please!'

A man begging, but she knew he fought the desire to smash his fist to her face, to beat her, to break her spirit and gain her submission. A man willing to kill for the sake of his child, the progeny she could have, the only immortality he would ever know.

'I'll want — '

'It's in the basement,' he said. 'Already installed. The best equipment on the market. If you want to change it or get more just give the word.'

'I'll need — '

'It's done. Inputs to all medical records, government statistics, industrial data banks, private stacks — ' His gesture encompassed the world. 'Name it and it's yours. Will you help me?'

'Sure — for ten million.'

'Dollars?' He hadn't expected the demand. 'Are you talking about money?'

'That's right.' She smiled, enjoying her triumph. 'What's wrong with money?'

7

In the dimness the figure was the concrete realization of the masturbatory fantasies Wolfe had known when growing into manhood. In the light it would have a face and hair and an expression which would give it both independence and individuality but, now, it was nothing but a mass of warm and female flesh which he could touch and fondle and use as he pleased.

'Sam?' Stirring she moved, one arm lifting to fall across his shoulders, her body turned to press the mounds of her breasts against his torso, the nipples small spears of irritation. 'Sam?'

Wolfe said, 'I'm here, Glenda.'

'Then come to me.' She began to nuzzle his upper arm. 'Come to me, darling.'

He moved away from her, regretting he had taken her to his bed, but how to resist the offer when it had been made so obvious? The nurses had grown stale aside from Avril Kinski who had left him in no doubt as to her feelings. For her all men were anathema. Glenda, hired to take care of Lynne Colman and her quarters, had provided novelty.

'Sam?'

'I'm thinking.' He kept his face turned from her wishing she would go back to sleep.

'About Celia?' She lifted herself on one elbow, fully awake now, tiny patches of brilliance reflected from her eyes. 'Is there any hope?'

'There's always hope.'

'But when? Such a lovely girl and her father with all that money.' Envy tinged her voice. 'I was surprised when I saw him. I thought he'd be much older but he's young enough to father a child and good-looking enough to find a scad of women who'd help him do it. There's a lot to be said for maturity.'

'Sure,' said Wolfe. 'That much more money.'

'There's more to life than money.' She sounded defensive. 'A woman needs love, too, and affection. A man who doesn't just think of her as something to be used. Most men are selfish. An older one knows how to take his time.' Her voice changed a little, 'Darling?'

'Relax.'

'Trouble?' She edged closer. 'Don't worry about it. But you're a doctor, couldn't you mix up a little something to, well, you know.'

'Sure. I'll take care of it tomorrow. I know just the thing. It'll do you the world of good.'

'Not for me, stupid!' Her hands grew busy. 'To wake you up, darling. To give you back some of that zip.' Her breath grew faster. 'Sam! Do something!'

He knew his anatomy. After a period of gasping she relaxed, sweating but satisfied.

'That was great, Sam. Where did you learn how to do things like that? The medical school?' She chuckled. 'You should work that way on Celia. Hell, with that technique you'd have a corpse kicking.' She sensed his anger. 'Did I say something wrong?'

'You said something stupid. If Max heard you he'd have your hide.'

'Maybe. But he might be too busy to hear me. I've seen the way Lynne Colman looks at him. The way he looks at her, too. You want to bet they aren't getting that way about each other?'

'You've a one-track mind.'

'I'm a realist and know what makes the world go round. How long is she going to stay here, anyway? It's been weeks now. Not that I'm complaining but I'd like to know how long the job will last.' Her lips drifted over his cheek.

'I'd miss you, darling.'

'It'll be mutual.'

'Do we have to part? I'm not exactly a nurse but I could look after Celia as good as they do. I'm used to taking care of people. I had to look after the kids when I was young, babies too. I've done my share of feeding and cleaning. From what I can make out Celia's not much different. Just a baby in a way. How about it, Sam, will you speak for me?'

'I'll do what I can.'

'You promise?'

'Sure.'

'When? Tomorrow?'

'Maybe.'

'Tomorrow,' she insisted. 'Sam — '

'Got to sleep,' he snapped. 'I'm tired.'

Feyman couldn't sleep. He threw the switch and leaned back listening to the, silence which followed the bedroom murmurings. Tomorrow the woman would leave — no one who could even entertain such thoughts as she'd voiced could be allowed near Celia. Wolfe? He was good and some license had to be made. As it had to be made with Kinski and her peccadilloes. People were not machines to be squeezed into a mold. As long as they were loyal and did what they were paid to do it was enough.

The switch moved beneath his hand; the study, Harman's room and the regular breathing of a man asleep. Celia's room and the soft rustle of the attendant nurse as she moved about the chamber on her business. Lynne's room was silent but from the basement he caught the sounds of the machines at work, the woman who operated them.

One who would walk out if she knew he spied on her.

He killed the speaker, regretting its use but aware of its necessity. The life he lived was edged with perils, money against money, the rich wanting to get richer at the expense of their own. Spies, industrial agents, saboteurs — he had known them all. Now that he had risen into the more stable field of established wealth the dangers were not so crude but only a fool neglected elementary precautions. A security corps monitored his activities — one owned by himself. Set to check up on those who worked for him as they were checked up on in turn. Layers of protection for the fortune he had created — for what?

To build monuments?

Blanche was gone and he could see again the wreck of the car in which she had died. Torn metal lying at the foot of a cliff, ugly marks where it had smashed the barrier as it had left the road, a smear of something that could have been blood but had been lubricant on the stone halfway down. A woman, complaining of neglect, finding refuge in dissipation. Why hadn't she been able to understand the business pressures that had kept him from her side?

Shamarre and Michael had been murdered. Feyman touched the scar of his wrist and thought again of the house and smoke and scattered debris which had greeted him when, late, he had returned home. An accident they had called it; a gas-explosion, but he had known better. Three years later those he had held responsible had died for their error in not making sure he had been with the others when they had triggered their bomb.

Now Celia.

Feyman closed his eyes, seeing her when she had been small and young and the promise of the future. Running towards him over a meadow dotted with yellow daisies. Laughing, screaming with pleasure as he had swept her up to whirl her high above his head before setting her gently down. An early memory followed by a stream of others as she had grown to take on her own personality. To choose her own way.

What had happened to her?

How long must he wait?

Feyman opened his eyes and reached for a button then froze the movement of his hand. Lynne Colman liked to work alone as she had made clear. Pressured she might explode to lapse into a sulky fit which could last for days. Or make a mistake they would both regret.

Rising he found the brandy and tucked it under his arm before picking up a couple of glasses. A gentleman, calling on a lady, should always bear gifts.

She was hard at work on the computer and he stood watching her from the door. She wore a loose robe of some thin, white material, and her arms and feet were bare. Her movements were deft, fast, precise. Those of a dancer then, watching, he corrected the impression.

Not a dancer but a priestess. One serving her modern god as her ancient sisters had served idols of wood and stone. The gestures that could have been genuflections or the intricate pattern of a ritual ceremony. The computer terminal was the altar, the buttons and keys the sacred seeds or stones that could predict future events. The litter of discarded printouts was the residue of sacrifice. The glare of overhead lights the modern equivalent of candles. And the incense?

Surely that must be her perfume.

Without turning she said, 'What's the matter, Max? Couldn't you sleep?'

'No. You?'

'When I've got my teeth into a problem I can't let it rest.' She swore as she hit the wrong key and slammed her palm against the cancel. 'Damn! I guess I'm not seeing straight.'

'You're tired. Give it a rest,'

'No. I've got this mother on the run and I'm seeing it through to the end.' She snarled as, again, she made a mistake. 'To hell with it. Is that booze you're carrying?'

She took the glass he handed to her and lifted it pursing her lips as she saw the amount he had poured. Then, with a shrug, she swallowed it, coughed, held out the glass for more.

'Here. Give me a refill while I find my pills.' They were blue, in a phial resting

97

among the litter of papers on her desk. Feyman watched as she shook out a couple and gulped them down with the brandy. She smiled as again he replenished her glass. 'Thanks. I like a man who knows what to do when it needs to be done. In a couple of minutes now I'll be as good as new.'

'You don't look too bad as you are.'

'You mean no bloodshot eyes, lank hair, haggard cheeks, slumped shoulders, trembling hands?' Her laughter was music. 'Fatigue comes from within — when you reach that state you're exhausted. I'm losing the fine edge of my coordination. That's the second time I loused up and I can't afford to make any mistakes.'

'Can't you incorporate a checking program?'

'Of course and I'll repeat the sequence, but now I'm heading for goal and to hell with anything which gets in my way.' She lifted the phial. 'You want?'

Feyman shook his head. 'You've found something?'

'Maybe.' She lifted her glass. 'Just maybe.'

Hope caught him, shaking his compo-
sure with unexpected force, blurring his
eyes and creating a thin singing in his
ears. A moment during which he sat
immobile then he drank and the brandy
stung his mouth and throat and he was
himself again; a man who didn't believe
in promises and who owned nothing until
it was in his hand.

'Are you sure?'

'No, but it's a chance. A good one.' She
guessed what he was thinking. 'It's not
what you hope it is,' she said quickly.
'I can't cure Celia and have never said I
could. Did Taro?'

'No. He just said that of the people
who could help me you were the one he
recommended.'

'Help,' she mused. 'How do you help a
man? You can't do it by carrying him on
your back and you can't do it by letting
him lean on you. In either case he can
only follow the path you take which leaves
him flat once you part. The only real way
to help a man is to give him strength, to
take him to the junction, teach him how
to read the signs and then to let him

make his own way. To force him to do it. Am I making sense?'

'Yes.'

'Good. Sometimes I go a little wild after souping up. That's why I'm waiting for the peak to flatten. Taro told you the answer had to be found within your own culture because that is the only one you can really understand. He should have added that the problem seems to be the result of that same culture.' She took a sip of her brandy. 'I ran that check I told you about — the run-down on each and every known victim. The result was a washout. Nada, zilch, zero — a pure random pattern spread all over. Nothing in common at all. More cases in heavily populated areas but too variable to make any kind of sense. In any case that's what you'd expect from a random pattern anyway.' She finished her drink and looked at the glass then set it down. 'I've had enough.'

'So you found nothing.'

'I eliminated a possibility,' she corrected. 'The cause of this thing can't be found by victim-comparison. What do you know about computers?'

She smiled at his frown.

'Most people think they're some kind of god-machine and others think they're just elaborate toys. Both are wrong. Once they used to say you couldn't do anything with a computer you couldn't do with a pencil and paper. That's true enough if you're just talking about calculators. A pencil, paper — and time. Computers are something else. Can you find the volume of a sphere? A cylinder? A trapezoid? A polyhedron?'

'No,' he admitted. 'I don't have formulae.'

'A computer does. All that and more stored in its memory banks so you ask and it delivers. That makes it a kind of super-library but there's more. A good computer can find the answers to questions you don't know how to ask. A good computer — with a top operator. The machine is only as good as the one using it.'

She was telling him something and he waited, watching, sensing that her drug-induced euphoria was dying. To interrupt would be to break her train of thought and ruin communication.

'The secret of success in our society is to be able to find the person who can do what needs to be done,' she continued. 'We're too specialized for our own good. All tucked away in our little compartments, each an expert in his field, an idiot out of it. You could waste years on research that has already been done. On designing a component which has been perfected and forgotten. Computers hold the answer. Not just to reclaim information but to find the answers to questions no one has ever bothered to ask. To use statistical analysis to find a node, to identify it, to take it apart to discover how it can be resolved.' She blinked and said, calmly, 'Well, that's enough lecturing for today. Let's see if I'm going to win the prize.'

She returned to the computer and Feyman revised his previous analogy. Not just a priestess serving an ancient god but one attending an oracle. Would the answers it gave be as ambiguous as those yielded by the Sybils?

'This is it.' She studied the printout, then frowned. 'Damn!'

'Something wrong?'

'You could say that.' Looking at him she explained. 'It's always a mistake to hope that something will be simple. I programmed the computer to deliver the name of the person most likely to be able to solve the problem. I'd hoped for one; we've got three. Tagholm, Devin and Moynihan. Devin can't be located. Tagholm's on Mars.'

'And Moynihan?'

'On the Moon. We'll try him first.'

8

They traveled light; Wolfe together with Minchin and the nurses attending Celia. If the cure for what ailed her waited on the Moon Feyman wanted her close. An accident; a thrombosis or coronary or stroke could rob him of the prize just when it was in his hand.

Owning his own zipship was an affectation in which he had never indulged. It was easier, cheaper and safer to charter as required and, if no ships were available for that, to empty a commercial-light vessel with bribes, compensation and bonuses. Always there was something extra for the captain.

It was John Lipman's turn to be lucky.

He watched the last of his Passengers climb the ramp and turned to face the control panel, waiting until the green light showed the hull to be sealed. Beside him his co-pilot Roy Heffer eased his bulk in the chair and rolled his gum from one side of his mouth to the other. A habit Lipman detested and he could have done without the after-shave the other wore which filled the cabin with a pungent odor. Not for the first time he considered putting in a request for another co-pilot then, as always, decided against it. Heffer was good at his job and to protest his habit of chewing gum would make him conspicuous and some idle bastard might take it into his head to question his own capabilities.

'Did you see her?' The gum gave a false resonance to Heffer's voice. 'All covered up and her face veiled. Those nurses, too. What are we carrying?'

'A man who'll stamp on you like a bug if you get too curious.' Lipman touched a button. To those in the salon he said, 'We are sealed and ready to depart. Please take your seats.'

A job the stewardess should have done but Mary had twisted her ankle when loading supplies and Feyman had refused to wait for a replacement. Not that one was necessary — on a milk run like this Lipman could handle everything alone, but if the union found he'd run crew-light there could be trouble.

'Captain? May I sit with you?'

Lynne Colman, smiling, moving into the cabin before he could object. He saw Heffer's raised eyebrows, his smile, then the flash of light on the panel put an end to possible argument.

'Five seconds to departure. Mark!'

A slight jerk and they were well away from the planet that hung like a blue-white ball beneath them. Another and it had became shrunken, the atmosphere a mist dotted with cloud, all features blurred and even the seas hard to determine. Yet another and stars blazed beyond the windows, cold, distant, watching like dispassionate eyes. The sun, shielded by the bulk of the Earth, haloed it with a flaring luminescence.

The Moon hung to one side, a silvered crescent blotched and marred with the shadows of what had once been thought to have been oceans. One of them, the Mare Ibrium, was their destination.

It came hurtling towards them, to hang

apparently motionless, shimmering in the screens.

Lynne said, 'What's the matter? Why don't we land?'

'Computer-block.' Lipman was terse. At times it happened but he wished this wasn't one of them. 'It's busy down there and we've been stacked to wait our turn. The computer's plotting our landing — we don't want to zipout at the same place and time as another ship.'

'It happens?'

'It can. That's why we radio a continuous signal. The tower picks it up, feeds it into their computer and the machine determines when we land. You want to get down fast?' He glanced at Heffer as she nodded. 'Roy?'

'Go ahead.'

A signal, she guessed, for the co-pilot to stay silent about what was to happen. Planned action with which he had agreed. She gasped as, suddenly, the Moon vanished to show an empty vista of stars. It appeared again, closer, vanishing to again reappear. She saw it no longer shimmered.

As they landed she said, 'That was neat.'

'Special service for special people.' Roy Heffer chewed his gum. 'Just for you and yours, honey.'

'You zipped the Moon,' she said. 'That way you re-registered with the tower and got a higher priority because you'd come in too close to be ignored. Right?'

Lipman said, 'Yes, but I hope you won't talk about it.'

'I won't.'

'Thanks. The company doesn't like it and you can guess how those in the tower feel. If you hire on a free charter we can zip all day if you want. The Moon, Venus, Mars, Mercury even. An inner-planet tour. Interested?'

'I'll think about it.'

'Let me know if you decide to try it.' Lipman hit a switch as the umbilical tube made contact with the hull. As a lamp flashed from red to green he said, 'Seal's tight. You can disembark now. Enjoy your stay.'

They'd arrived as the terminator bisected the area; one half bright beneath naked sunlight, the other dark aside from the reflection of stars. A busy time, the installation was thronged with tourists eager to witness the spectacle, lingering beneath the transparent domes and promenades until the terminator had reached the horizon and the long night closed in.

Installed in the Armstrong Hotel Feyman joined Lynne Colman, waited as she used the phone. The communication-net was good; within seconds she was talking to a plump-faced woman at Archimedes.

'I really must see him. I've come all the way from Mars and my husband will never forgive me unless I take him back one of his pieces. It is the right man, isn't it? Moynihan? Cyril Moynihan? The famous sculptor?'

'We do have a sculptor, on the third tier. His name, yes, Cyril Moynihan.'

'Please connect me. I really must speak to him. This is such an exciting time for me.'

A pause then, 'I'm sorry but the gentleman is not available at this time.'

'Where is he?' Lynne mollified her tone. 'Can I contact him? My itinerary doesn't give me much time and it's so terribly important that I speak with him. When will he be back?'

'A day or two. Maybe more — I'm not certain. He comes and goes as the feeling takes him.'

She shrugged and Feyman remembered the stubborn independence of off-worlders, a deserved reputation and, from what he'd learned, Moynihan was far from cooperative.

'Could you please record a message for him?' Lynne smiled at the screen. 'I would be so grateful. Tell him an old friend of his, Jud Pastern, has been asking after him. If I can't manage to see him I'll let Jud know where he is and he can call for me. If he gets in touch soon, it won't matter, but I'll only be at the Armstrong for a few days.'

Feyman waited until she had broken the connection.

'Who the hell is Jud Pastern?'

'Moynihan spent some time with him about twenty years ago. They were both mercenaries in the Guatemalian fringe-war. You remember that?' As he nodded she continued, 'They were guidance technicians and helped to flatten the Santa Anna complex. Later both were proscribed as criminal activists. Pastern did time but Moynihan won clear.'

'Legally?'

'No.'

'So you're using a little pressure,'

'Why not? We need him. Now what shall we do while waiting for him to call?'

They started with dinner, eating in a circular room capped with transparency. Earth would soon dominate the sky, now it held a ghostly distortion as if it was the ghost of a planet, one ravaged by furious energies. After a dessert of feather-light cake loaded with succulent cream they sipped liqueurs and bandied conversation. The first real opportunity they'd had; within the house, work had dominated every waking hour.

He said, 'How did you become what you are?'

'Don't you know?' She smiled as he made no answer. 'Is that why you invited me to dinner? To probe my murky past?'

She had dressed for the occasion in a long gown of dusty red material the fabric edged and ornamented with golden filigree. Barbaric splendor accentuated by the gold she wore around her neck, at her ears, on her wrists. Cosmetics enhanced her lips, the bones of her cheeks, her deep-set eyes. Around her hung a cloud of exotic perfume; odors which brought concepts of orchids and sunlight and the deep, dreaming shadows of jungle nights.

'You know about me, Max. All you had to do was to ask and you must have done just that. My parents, early years, upbringing, educational accomplishments — it's all a matter of record. I had an early love for computers. I guess I liked their precision so I tended to work with them more and more. The rest — ' She made a gesture with a slender hand. 'As I say it's a matter of record.'

'What you've done, yes,' he agreed. 'But not why you did it. What happened at Lanchester? Why did you leave the Cullimin Foundation? Why did you run to the Belt?'

'Run?' She met his eyes. 'Who said I ran?'

'The project you were on was routine. Your talent was wasted on it. The Belt isn't the most comfortable place to be and even Ceres leaves a lot to be desired.' He paused then said, gently, 'Did you love him so much?'

'Damn you, Max Feyman!'

'For asking what I did?'

'For making me remember the past.' She drank her liqueur then, looking at the empty glass, she smiled. 'No, you're right, it's impossible to run away. Your memories go with you just as your skin does. Ghosts waiting to greet you no matter where you wind up. I guess we both have enough of those.'

Feyman lifted a hand, caught a waiter's attention, signaled for more drinks.

'It was a man,' she said. 'For me he became the universe. I admired, respected, loved him.'

'Sagoo Brice.' Feyman picked up his new drink and looked at it. 'A lecturer at Lanchester. Moved to the Cullimin Foundation when he gained his doctorate. Volunteered for the Brandt-Hartley Expedition. They've been gone how long now? Three years? Two?'

'Three.'

'You waited then ran to the Belt. Right?'

She said, with sudden anger, 'You know too damned much! Why ask if you know the answers? And why look for them anyway?'

'You work for me,' he said. 'You're close to Celia.' Two good reasons and one would have been enough. 'Why didn't you marry him?'

'Once I was about to but things happened and we delayed the ceremony. Then I became too busy. And when tests showed I'd become sterile there didn't seem to be any point.'

'No? You surprise me.'

'Because I associate marriage with children? What other reason can there be for it? A couple can live together without a civil contract or a religious blessing if they want — but children are something else. If you don't want them or can't have them why get married and risk the pain of later divorce?'

'Some get married for life.'

'Some — maybe, but how many make it?' She lifted her own drink and swallowed it and rose with sudden impatience. 'Let's get out of here.'

The terminator had passed and they walked beneath transparencies decorated with the blazing vista of the cosmos the splendor a background to the majesty of Earth. Music stirred the air from small orchestras set in unexpected enclaves, the live, muted strains together with the oddly bizarre costumes of the players providing a titivation for ear and eye.

Other music pulsed from underground caverns; sonorous chords accompanied by drifting swathes of vibrant color. Here the old custom of bodily contact had been reintroduced and Feyman could feel the soft warmth of his partner as he held her close to him; the cushions of her breasts, the firm strength of her hips and thighs. Her eyes came almost level to his own. In them he read the same hunger that had grown to possess him, the same need.

Later they strolled through a garden graced with delicate fronds and intricate blooms. A paradise that held the tinkle of water from a variety of sources. And later still they strolled along a promenade flanked with crystal through which could be seen the bleak harshness of the exterior world. Rock and dust and barren emptiness, the loom of distant mountains, the endless plain of the Mare Imbrium itself marked and blotched with countless craters.

Had Celia looked at such a view? She had been at Tycho but the vista was much the same and the interior facilities followed a pattern. Water, gardens, music, caverns, promenades — things fashioned as if to bring something of familiar comfort to a hostile environment. A poetic concept but he knew the pattern was dictated by the needs of survival and the seeming artistry merely a façade.

At his side Lynne Colman said, 'Why did men ever leave the beauty of home for this?'

'Because it was here.'

'Boys,' she said. 'Always itching to peer over the next mountain. Always wanting to know what's in the next field.'

'And girls,' he said. 'Waiting at home to comfort them when they return.'

'If they return.' Her voice was bitter. 'Sometimes they don't.'

He waited, sensing her need to talk.

'He loved me,' she said. 'He told me that often and he wasn't lying. He did love me — but he loved something else even more. Adventure, I guess you'd call it, and when he was invited to join the Brandt-Hartley Expedition to Pluto he couldn't refuse. So he left and I waited. In a sense I'm still waiting. They were never heard from after they passed the orbit of Neptune.'

'If he returned?'

'Now? Nothing. It's too late.' She drew in her breath and exhaled with a sharp gusting. 'Memories,' she said. 'They can be hell.'

Something he knew too well and she guessed it as he led her back to the hotel and their rooms. As if by accident their hands met and clung and something of the emotion they had both felt while dancing rose to lock them in a common bond.

'Lynne, I — '

'Max!' Her free hand rose to rest fingers lightly on his lips. 'We're both adult. We know what it's about. There's only one question — your room or mine?'

The phone settled the question. They heard it ring from her room as they approached. It was Archimedes calling. Moynihan would be at home in an hour.

9

A crawler took them to the complex, dropping them at the main entry, Feyman paying the admission tax which covered their use of air. Arms ran from the serrated dome in long extensions running along the rim of the crater; promenades which gave magnificent views and which were backed by rows of shops, kiosks, restaurants, bars, fun-palaces and the like. Most were of standard construction using sheeted plastic, others utilized local materials to fashion outré façades of ridges, planes, half-seen faces, eyes which winked and lips which curved in enticing smiles.

Moynihan's place was unmistakable.

Lynne paused as they neared it, halting to stare at the swell and curve of artfully fashioned stone. The façade was that of a woman, kneeling, the view from the rear so that her naked buttocks swelled over parted thighs. The space between

119

contained the door.

She said, 'I wonder how many passing through it don't look up?'

Those that did saw their reflection in a mirror. A subtle jest betraying Moynihan's opinion of his customers as they came and went. A part of his calculated image as was the stained pants and smock he wore, the sandals, the short beard, the single jewel dangling from his left ear.

'A moment.' He waved to them as they entered. 'Look around and be patient. I'll be with you as soon as I've finished robbing these innocents.'

The couple facing him were young, gratified at having met a 'character', willing to swallow his insults and not believing half of what he said. After more banter they paid for the statuette he lauded and left with their prize. It, like almost everything else in the shop, had been made of ground rock mixed with a polymer binding. Feyman picked up a similar article and noted the way it had been curved and molded.

'Hand made,' said Moynihan. 'Like everything else you see. No two are alike but some are pretty close so you could find a near-match if your taste runs that way. If it does you're in the wrong place. Try the shop a dozen places along and say I sent you. I can use the commission.'

He was a big man now running to fat. His russet hair was spiked and his eyes, gray, rested in a mesh of lines. His forehead was low and sloped sharply backward. His hands were large, the nails grimed. He smelt of sweat and chemicals. A man who drank and smiled too much.

He lost the smile as Lynne said, 'You are expecting us. The friends of Jud Pastern, remember?'

'So you're the ones.' Moynihan looked past them at the door. 'A moment while I lock up.' As he rejoined them he said, curtly, 'What's all this crap about?'

'We just thought you'd like to know about your old friend.'

'He's no friend of mine.'

'No?' Lynne drew her finger over a table and lifted it thick with dust. 'Been on a vacation?'

'A business trip.' His leer was unmistakable. 'A personal matter,'

'Which you broke off in a hurry. What brought you back?'

'I can't sell if I'm not here.'

'Or find out about Jud,' She moved around the shop, touching, examining, lifting a delicate figurine. It was carved from a block of some translucent material and depicted a young girl standing, head thrown back, arms extended from her sides. Her hair was a rippling cascade and artistic magic had given her features an expression of vibrant life. 'This is good. Did you make it?'

'I make it all. What about Jud?'

'This too?' She ignored his question. The piece she touched was crudely primitive in its lack of detail but, even so, it held a raw appeal. 'Where did you get the idea for it? Guatemala?'

'Where's that?'

'You should know. They remember you there. The Santa Anna complex — Jud always figured he had a raw deal. Somehow he thinks you sold him out. I think he'd very much like to meet up with you. Shall I tell him where to find you?'

Moynihan said, thickly, 'You bitch!'

'Try again.'

'What the hell do you want?'

'That's better. All we want is a little help. In return I'll give you some good news. Jud Pastern is dead. He died two years ago in Honolulu.' Lynne looked at the sculptures. 'Some of these are quite good, Cyril. How much are you making?'

For a moment Feyman thought the man would attack her and tensed; then, abruptly, Moynihan bellowed with laughter.

'Jesus, you had me going there! Jud dead, you say? It's no joke?'

'Not as far as he's concerned.'

Moynihan laughed again. 'By God a woman with a sense of humor. Marry me, darling, and I'll give you half of what I own. A drink?'

He produced a bottle and glasses, poured, gulped his down before Feyman had tasted his own. The man was over-reacting, sure proof of the strain he'd been under and which Lynne had calculated to a hair. But how could he help Celia?

Moynihan shrugged as, bluntly, he put the question.

'I don't know. I'm sorry to hear about your girl but I haven't a clue as to how to help her. She isn't the only one, you know. There's a clinic at Eratosthenes that's full of them — Anholt runs it. Maybe he could help.'

Lynne shook her head as Feyman looked at her. 'We've checked that out. All he can offer is care and we can handle that ourselves. Have you seen many zombies?'

'One was enough. It was maybe a dozen years ago when I first set up here. A party was out climbing and they had some trouble. I went out with a few others and brought them back. One had zombied.'

'His name?'

'Franz Heinman. A loner. He died soon afterwards.'

'Died?'

'That's what I said.' Moynihan met her eyes. 'He caught something and clocked out. Don't ask me what — it happened a long time ago.'

'But you remember his name.'

'It was all the poor bastard left behind

him. The rest went on expenses. On the books he just died from natural causes. This was a new development, you understand, and those behind it didn't want any trouble. A man turning zombie like that was bad publicity so they buried it.' Moynihan paused, brooding. 'I had trouble sleeping for a while after it happened. I kept seeing those empty, staring eyes.'

Lynne waited until the man had drunk and refilled his glass.

'Have you seen others since?'

'A few but I try to stay clear. I had one in the shop a while back but got those with him out fast. God alone knows why they brought him here in the first place. Maybe they hoped something would trigger a response but he just stood there like a corpse and, well, I guess you know all about that. But I got to thinking and wondered what could have caused a thing like that. Franz, now, he was in a suit and roped and everything. Others were with him and they weren't affected. They knew nothing until they tried to get him to move and even then they didn't know he'd zombied. His filters were dark and they couldn't see his face. At first they thought he'd had a heart attack or something and just died. It would have been better if he had.'

A victim buried and forgotten, forgotten for the sake of convenience. There could well be others.

'A light,' said Moynihan. He took another drink and reached unsteadily for the bottle. 'Watching him I used to think of a light. Where does it go when you flip the switch? You ever thought of that?'

The whiskey he was drinking was strong and this trip to the bottle wasn't his first. Strain and fear would have driven him to find liquid courage as relief had caused him to celebrate. Now the thickening of his voice showed he'd reached the edge.

'A light,' he said again. 'Maybe that's the answer. Maybe God just flipped the switch.'

And, maybe, the man knew more than he'd admitted. Feyman watched him as he set down the glass before making a swaying progress towards the rear of the shop. Lynne shook her head as he made to follow.

'Leave him, Max.'

'Has he helped?'

Her shrug was his answer. Feyman fought his disappointment wondering just what he'd hoped to gain. A miracle? Moynihan to have smiled and then produced an instant cure? Why had the computer delivered his name?

The man's absence irritated him and Feyman began to wander around the shop. A rapping at the door caught his attention. Three people were outside and frowned when he shook his head. The eldest, a thickset man, pointed at his wristwatch and lifted his eyebrows. Feyman held up both hands, fingers extended. If they wanted to return at ten Moynihan might be sober enough to serve them.

Lynne said, 'Sit down, Max. Take it easy.'

'I can't.'

He moved on, looking, touching, seeking relief in physical action. A large sculpture stood in a corner half-covered by drapes and he pulled them aside to reveal the writhing body of a tormented woman. Facing it he wondered how the artist worked. Did he get drunk, close his eyes and caress the hardening material as if he caressed the body of a woman? The shape hinted of something like that and Feyman stood close to it, resting his hands on it, following the sweeping curves, the deeper indentations. A woman, yes, but one with subtle distortions that removed pleasure from the touch. Had Moynihan's subconscious taken over to guide his hands to produce a depiction of what he had helped cause to be? The death and ruin and devastation born of his missiles fired during that vicious war twenty years ago?

He stepped back from the image as Lynne said, 'He's taking too long. Something could be wrong. Go and see what's keeping him.'

'He's drunk.'

'Please.'

The door to the rear stood ajar and he pushed it open. Beyond lay a workroom with the expected furnishings; a large table a potter's wheel, bins left beneath mechanical mixers, sacks of finely powdered stone. Sealed cartons of polymer resins stood on a wide shelf together with an assortment of metallic dyes. Coils of wire for armatures were stacked in a corner and another held a head of moulds.

A spray gun and paints stood racked onto one wall. Dust was everywhere. The air held a harsh, acrid taint and the floor was gritty beneath his feet.

Moynihan was nowhere in sight.

Feyman moved to the far end of the room where another door broke the surface of a wall. It gave onto a small chamber that led to a kitchen, empty, the table littered with assorted cans and fragments. The bedroom held a wide, double bed, some cabinets, a hypnotic sleep-inducer and a softly rich carpet. A bathroom led from it containing a tub, a shower, a washbowl and toilet facilities. Moynihan sat on the edge of the tub, his face in the washbowl, vomit thick around the drain.

'Cyril?'

Feyman touched him, feeling the

flaccidity of the throat, the pulse surging beneath the skin. A bottle lay on its side against the wall and the air held the reek of whiskey over the taint of vomit. Some pills in a plastic container were clutched in the artist's hand.

Feyman returned to the bedroom. The drawers of the cabinets yielded nothing of interest and he closed them before, frowning, he looked around. Moynihan was important, why? A man named by the computer as one who could have the cure he was seeking or, at least, knowledge of the cause of what afflicted Celia. A drunken artist living in fear and getting a jag from pills. One now lying stoned and heedless.

If he had the answer where would it be?

Books spilled from a rack all containing the kind of text and pictures he had assumed would be Moynihan's choice.

Feminine garments frothed from a secret drawer beneath the bed. Tapes that filled the hypnotic-inducer screen with the writhing of endless copulations. A notebook containing numbers. A photograph that was not what he expected.

Feyman lifted it, frowning. It was in full color and showed a vista as seen from a Jovian satellite; Io, Ganymede, Europa or just a shot of the giant planet taken from space. One of a series depicting the wonders of the Solar System.

Taped to its back was a card and he frowned as he read the name.

'Max?'

'Coming.' Lynne stood in the work-room. He shrugged as he met her eyes. 'Our friend is drunk and riding high. Pills. He's on a way-out trip.'

'Why?'

'Maybe he didn't like to answer questions. Or maybe he was scared you'd turn him in anyway. Or he could have been paid to stay under cover and felt his world begin to crack wide open.' He handed her the photograph and card.

'Why should Jafek Furneaux be interested in Moynihan?'

'If he is.'

'That's his card.'

'It's a card with his name printed on it,' she corrected. 'Do you know him?'

'We've had dealings.'

'And?'

'I'm still curious to know what connection there could be between him and Moynihan.'

'Maybe there's none.' Lynne's tongue showed between her teeth as she peeled the card from the back of the photograph. 'What are you going to do about our friend?'

'Forget him.'

'You mean to leave him as he is?'

'What else? He's done all this before. He'll sleep and dream and be sick if he has to then he'll recover enough to fall into bed. Just forget him.'

She said, dubiously, 'I don't think we should. The computer gave his name as one who could help.'

'He's a drunk. Maybe the computer didn't know that. Maybe he could have helped us before he started hitting the bottle and getting a jag from pills. Now he's useless. We've just wasted out time.'

'Maybe not.' Smiling she held out the photograph. In the space which the card had covered was scrawled a few words and a name. 'It's a message from Devin,' she said. 'He's on Ganymede.'

10

Feyman had gone and it was his night to howl. Wolfe looked back once at the closed door of the suite then concentrated on his own intentions. With Minchin on watch, nurses on standby and Avril Kinski in immediate attendance Celia was as safe as she could ever be. He had made his check and a bleeper would summon him if he was needed. Now was his chance to escape the confines of the Armstrong Hotel.

'Doctor?' A man accosted him as he headed for the doors leading into the complex beyond. 'Doctor Sam Wolfe?'

'That's right.'

'Anholt. Doctor Anholt.' He was a small, neat man with alert, brown eyes. His skin held the rich warmth of molten chocolate. His hair was grizzled and a scar puckered the cheek below and to the left of his right ear.

As Wolfe touched the fingers of his

proffered hand he said:

'I own the clinic over at Eratosthenes. You may have heard of it. A small place but I like to think one of the finest on Luna.'

'The one dealing with geriatric cases? Yes, I've heard of it.'

'I'd like you to pay us a visit if you have the time.'

'Thank you, Doctor. I'll think of it.'

'Tony,' said Anholt. 'My friends call me Tony.'

'Sam.' Wolfe smiled as they established their relationship. 'You must be doing well.'

'I am.' Anholt smiled in return but there was more to the smile than a display of pleasure. Wolfe recognized it, the professional man-to-man signal. 'The old come to me and I give them the best of care and, in return, they live on and on and on. No stress, you understand. A sheltered environment and the low gravity all contribute to greater efficiency of debilitated organs. Hearts last longer, lungs, the spleen and kidneys — but you know all about that. I've patients who came to me as terminal cases a decade ago and who are in better health now than they were then. I've even got a couple well past the hundred mark who want to get married again. Why not — they have the right.'

And, as long as they had the money, Anholt would provide them with a place to live and the best of care. Wolfe knew what would happen to his charges if they outlived their funds.

He said, 'All this is very interesting, Tony, but some other time, eh? I'm hoping to grab a little off-duty relaxation.'

'And you shall, Sam! You shall. How about trusting an old Selenite to show you around? What were you thinking of doing? Visiting the Mirror Room? The Bowl? Trying your luck at the tables?'

'Something like that.'

'I thought so, but why here? There's some real action where the maintenance crews hang out.'

'I'll manage.' Wolfe resented being pressured. 'There's no need to look far. Good food, pleasant surroundings, congenial company — and one way of losing your money is as good as the next. Be seeing you, Tony.'

'Wait!' Anholt caught at his arm. 'I wonder if we could talk?'

'Here?' Wolfe glanced at the doors, the complex beyond. It followed the usual pattern; a curved roof set with lights, a smooth floor, walls pierced at intervals with openings. Above them glowed signs giving directions.

Others advertised various establishments. Wolfe was eager to visit them. 'Why don't you just give me a ring?'

It was his turn to pressure and Anholt recognized it. He said, smiling, 'Let me buy you dinner. I guess you could eat, right? Let's try the Bowl. You'll like it.'

It was as its name implied; a semi-hemisphere ringed by tiers of seats, the base a stage on which a naked girl was dancing. She was tall, lithe, gymnastic and, aided by a blend of glowing lights and drum-music gave a skillful if routine performance.

'A little goes a long way,' said Anholt as he glanced at her. 'But it's early yet. Later they really let their hair down. Will you

136

allow me to do the ordering?'

The food was sauced and spiced, the wine chilled and potent, the entertainment growing progressively more lewd and explicit. Wolfe ignored it, wondering why Anholt had waited to accost him; the meeting could have been no accident. Wondered too why the man was so eager to please.

'You are a colleague,' said Anholt when, bluntly, Wolfe put the question. 'A visitor to the Moon. Is it so unusual for one member of the profession to offer hospitality to another?'

Wolfe said, dryly, 'Where I come from you check for scalpels in the back after being entertained by strangers. Especially by one who just happened to be standing around when you made an appearance. How far is your clinic from here? Or maybe you came looking for a partner — haven't I heard you're under financial pressure?'

'No, Sam, you didn't hear that.' Anholt paused then added, 'What you may have heard is that I'm looking for a treatment to cure zombies.'

'Aren't we all?'

'That is why I contacted you. We have a mutual interest. At Eratosthenes I have many of the unfortunates in my care, some of them members of highly influential families. Sir Hugh Ragin, Lady Conway, the daughter of Samuel Haines, young Brad Eumillian, Donato Macari, Saeed Furneaux — you realize, naturally, I give you these names in the strictest confidence.'

And wanted — what? Leaning back in his chair, oblivious of the half-dozen couples locked in intricate copulation at the base of the Bowl, Wolfe could guess. Anholt was an entrepreneur of medicine. A high-flyer who'd used and could still be using plastic and manipulative surgery to win a fortune instead of to heal. His clinic gave him the opportunity to batten onto the old — now he hoped to hit the jackpot with a cure for zombies. Once he has it he could charge as much as the traffic would bear.

'You've a highly respected clinic,' said Wolfe. 'The relatives of those people you mentioned must really feel they can trust you.'

'As you can.' Anholt signaled for another bottle of wine. As he poured he said, 'There's a fortune in it. You see, I am blunt. Those who send those poor unfortunates to me would pay anything to have them cured. As your employer, Max Feyman, would give anything to have Celia herself again. He's behind you, isn't he? You could demand anything you wanted and he wouldn't argue. If you even had a hint of how a cure might be affected he'd see that it was checked out no matter what the cost.'

As would Furneaux. Had Ganter recommended Anholt to him? Were they splitting fees? It was possible but Wolfe doubted it; it was more probable that Furneaux had followed the example of others and handed the boy over to Anholt to see what he could do. He had simply left him there while he followed other lines of enquiry.

'You appreciate the situation,' said Anholt. 'If I could announce a cure and prove it on some of my patients it would be a momentous breakthrough. Naturally those associated with me would share in the glory and the financial rewards. More wine?'

'Why not?' Wolfe watched as his glass filled with sparkling delight. 'What's the problem?'

'Unfortunately I am still uncertain as to a few aspects of my research and lack the funds to have them pursued. The correlation, for example, I am certain there must be a common factor but which it is eludes me. You would eliminate food, I imagine? And water? Clothing and associated medication? Marital status and personal addiction to permitted drugs such as alcohol and caffeine and nicotine? Local and general influences? And yet, when all is eliminated, what is left?'

'Very little.'

'But something. There has to be something.'

Wolfe picked up his glass and looked at the bubbles. On the stage the fornicating couples had left to be replaced by a team of jugglers.

'There is something,' he admitted. 'It could lead to a cure.'

'And you are working to find it. You

and Max Feyman and — ' A pause which Wolfe ignored. 'Do you have a clue as to what the cure might be?'

Wolfe smiled and sipped his wine and said, 'You understand that any cure I might find would belong to Feyman? So even if I wanted to I couldn't possibly pass it on to you.'

'I understand the legalities. The cure would be his because he funded the research. You would get nothing he chose not to give. A pity, don't you agree?' Anholt smiled as Wolfe nodded. 'I see we understand each other. Yet ways can be found to circumvent the problem. I have a well-equipped laboratory at my clinic and, if when I get it, the discovery should be announced from Eratosthenes — you see my point?'

No connection or, at least, none that could be proved. Yet the very precaution advocated would leave Wolfe out in the cold and at the mercy of Anholt's generosity if he agreed to what the other proposed. Not that he had any intention of agreeing.

'Sam?'

Anholt was anxious. Wolfe, smiling, eased his concern. 'If anything comes up I'll remember you,' he promised. 'You know, this is really a nice wine. Were you going to order another bottle?'

It was late when they left the Bowl to part with mutual expressions of good will. Wolfe, aware of his condition, made his way to a pharmacy where sobup pills took care of his intoxication. A sauna helped to revive his general condition and soon he felt ready to test his luck on various games of chance. But one chance he didn't want to take. His bleeper hadn't sounded but if anything had happened and the instrument had malfunctioned and Feyman discovered he'd been out on the juice with Anholt his career would be over. It was best to make a check before heading for the casino.

He heard the song as he neared the door of Celia's room.

'Baby, baby, bunting
Daddy's gone a-hunting
For to get a rabbit skin
To wrap poor baby bunting in.'

'Doctor?' Minchin rose from where

he'd been sitting in a winged chair. 'Something wrong?'

'Just checking.' Wolfe nodded towards the closed door. 'Avril's got a fine voice.'

She turned as he entered, cheeks flushed, eyes bright, figure trim in her uniform. A bitch, thought Wolfe dispassionately. Displaying what she had no intention of ever yielding to one of his sex. But she was good at her job and was probably an even more conscientious guardian than Minchin. The reason Feyman continued to employ her.

'Doctor?'

'Just checking.' He moved to where Celia was sitting at the side of the bed. She wore a loose gown and Avril had obviously been getting her ready for her bath. 'More washing?'

'She must be kept clean, Doctor. Your own orders.'

He made no comment. 'No improvement as yet, I see. A pity. Well, carry on, Nurse Kinski. Sing to her all you want if you think it will help.' He added, dryly, 'But don't overdo the bathing.'

She waited until he had left before

returning to her charge. Gently she urged the girl to her feet and slipped the robe from her shoulders. Naked, the muscles flaccid beneath the skin, she seemed more pathetic than when dressed. All the elements of a superb beauty were present but the one thing that would have given unity to the whole was absent.

Only the hair, tended and brushed to a rich sheen, held the old attractiveness. The rest, like a smudged painting, held only a hint of what had been.

'Come with me, darling.' Avril's voice was a soothing purr. 'Come with me to the bath. That's right. One leg after the other. You're doing fine. Come to me, Celia. Come to me.'

How to God she wished she would. To come lovingly, willingly, eager to share the pleasure their mutual embrace could yield. But the face remained expressionless, the shoulders slumped, the blue eyes vacant, the gait awkward, the hands, dangling, uncaring.

The nurse's own trembled as she touched the soft smoothness of the naked skin, pushing to guide, pressing, resisting the temptation to rove over the curves. The tub, prepared, stood before them. Mist rose from the scented water; a vapor which swirled as Celia stepped into the bath. As the water lapped around her calves she swayed, half-turned then, without warning, slumped and fell into the tub, a shower of water rising in a fountain of drenching rain.

'My God!' Avril dashed moisture from her eyes. 'Celia! Are you hurt, darling? Celia!'

She lay as she had fallen, face down in the water, hair trailing, legs slightly parted. Instantly the nurse was turning her, lifting her head free of the water, ignoring her own soaking condition.

'Celia!'

She was, thank God, unhurt. A foot must have turned, to ruin her precarious balance at a critical time. But if her face had hit the edge of the tub!

Avril felt sickened at the thought of it. The nose broken, the teeth, the lips split, and oozing blood. The skull fractured, bone driven into the brain — irreparable damage to add to the rest. But it hadn't happened and she was thankful for it.

'Stay as you are, darling.' She moved the girl's arms and thrust a floating sponge beneath her chin. 'I won't be a moment.'

Her uniform was soaked. To remove it was the work of a moment. A moment of hesitation and her underwear followed. Naked she returned to her charge.

'Now, honey, let's get you all nice and clean. Then I'll dry you and powder you all over and then take care of your hair and put you to bed. Up, now, darling. Up!'

Water splashed but it didn't matter and even added to the pleasure of the occasion as if they were two children sporting in a pool. The soap and sponge and the suds: which formed shielding bubbles. The rinse and toweling and dressing the girl in a robe. Another to cover her own nudity.

Hands caressing the gleaming hair with deft strokes of a brush.

Her voice, softer now, tremulous, whispering an old lullaby,

'Baby, baby bunting

Daddy's gone a-hunting
For to find a rabbit skin
To wrap poor baby bunting in.'
Then the tears, falling, wetting the
brush, the hair, the backs of her hands.

11

Seen from Ganymede Jupiter dominated the sky; a massive orb striped and banded with swathes of color, blotched by the giant Red-spot which always reminded Eric Tonge of a watching eye. He was a thin man with a sour face and a disposition to match, cursing the day he ever decided to become a traffic control officer and disgusted with himself for ever having left the inner worlds.

The job on Ganymede paid well but there was more to life than money and he could have done without that damned eye.

Leaning back in his chair he glared up at it. The control room was domed with transplast, the material treated to eliminate reflections, and it was easy to forget it was there. Beyond lay the void, the mass of winking lights denoting traffic, the bulk of giant storage tanks and the loom of Jupiter itself. Unseen, because it was scattered over the immediate terrain, was the wreckage created by a recent multiple-collision over field Beta 2 — the reason for the extra pressure and his growing headache.

'Steve!' He snarled at a colleague. 'For Christ's sake! You've fed an interloper into my sector!'

'Not guilty, man. He's a stranger,'

Tonge slammed his hand on a button and engaged the general channel. 'Warning,' he snapped. 'Any ship jumping instructions will be impounded and confiscated. No excuses. If you're guilty zipout now!'

Lights died on his screen as some obeyed. A few of those left were taking a chance and maybe they would get away with it but not if he could help it. Lax obedience to control had led to the debacle over Beta 2 and he was in no mind to tolerate cowboys. Let the bastards wait or take what was coming!

'Maintain pattern!' Steve Macary's voice lost some of its usual cool. 'X318 come in now. Two minutes to make landing. ZH4520 hold position. FA25 zipout and return in three minutes. Stacked vessels drop in sequence through corridor. Gamma 3? Any clear space your way?' He grunted at the negative answer. 'Do what you can.'

They were all doing just that but with a third of capacity knocked out it wasn't going to be enough. Tonge checked board and screen then twisted in his chair to look at the chief. Banter, old, his eyes pouched, jowls sagging, lifted his eyebrows.

'We'll have to scatter, Chief,' said Tonge. 'Get them out and down away from the area.'

'They'll love you for that.' Banter shrugged as Tonge expressed his opinion of their concern. 'I agree but we have to do what we can. Some of those boys must be low on air by now. Check situations and grant priorities.' He anticipated the objection. 'Just do it, Eric. And go easy on the threats, uh? Remember who pays our wages.'

A greedy bastard but good, thought Banter as Tonge turned back to his panel. And if he hadn't been greedy he would never have come to the Jovian System in the first place. None of them would; the controllers, the pilots, the companies and cowboys, the entrepreneurs, the gamblers and harlots and all the other damned parasites. Some, like the dredgers, risked their lives but most stood to lose little but their comfort. Well, to hell with it, a couple more years and he'd be set to retire.

Ivor Vale was a long way from that. He was young and fairly new still needing to develop the sharp edge held by the others. He sat at his board, hearing, but not listening to, the humming sussuration of instructions and reports that filled the room. A trick every controller quickly learned; his ears trained to respond only to personally applicable data.

Now they pricked to an outside signal.

'Chief!' he turned to wave at Banter. 'A radio message from Luna. Max Feyman's landing here in a chartered ship.'

'Feyman?' Banter pursed his lips. 'A wheel, uh? Check his ETA and do all you can to make him happy.'

Even in a zipship the journey took

time. Jupiter had been at superior conjunction on the far side of the sun and they'd had to rise high above the plane of the ecliptic to avoid the primary. A trip of over six hundred million miles and what with the normal procedures it would take more than a day. Time to eat, to shower, to rest in the empty lounge. Time to talk.

'This is traveling in style.' Lynne was enjoying the luxury. 'At least we've room to move. When I went out to the Belt I had to squeeze in with a couple of hundred others.'

Feyman made no comment. He sat on one of the seats looking through a side port and the illumination of the distant sun caught and limned his profile so that, watching, Lynne was reminded of some old carvings she had seen depicting an ancient Hittite king. He had the same hawk-like cast of features; the strong nose, the determined chin, the forehead, the savage eyes. A face that belonged on a coin. One adorned with a crown.

She said, quietly, 'Don't pin your hopes too high. Devin could turn out to be as useless as Moynihan.'

'So much for computers.'

His tone was flat and he didn't turn his head to look at her but she had no doubt as to his real meaning. How often had she told him that a computer was no better than its operator?

'Max.' She stepped forward, one hand lifting as of its own volition, reaching to touch his hair, to caress his cheek. Intimacy born from what had passed between them. 'Any regrets?'

'No.'

'Sure?'

'Why should there be?'

'It happens. Guilt at having betrayed your dead wife for example.' Her fingers moved to touch his lips. 'At having betrayed Celia.'

He said, 'I've been married twice. Did I betray my first wife by taking a second? Of course not. And, as for Celia — '

She waited for him to continue then, when he remained silent, said, 'Yes, darling? What about her? She must be intelligent enough to understand your need for a woman. In any case the problem has yet to arise.'

And maybe it never would — a thought that lifted him from the chair and sent him to pace the salon like a caged animal. Was she still well? Had there been any sudden deterioration? What if she had died while he had been locked in Lynne's embrace?

'Stop it, Max!' She caught his arm and forced him to a halt with unsuspected strength. 'Quit blaming yourself. No matter what may have happened to Celia you aren't responsible. In no way can you be blamed.'

'If she hadn't gone to the Moon — '

'She did. Are you God to determine what people should and should not do? Are you God not to have human needs? Human failings? You're doing all you can. Will your loneliness find a cure? Your pain? And aren't there others needing your concern?'

Herself for one. She had given him the comfort of her body and, in return, he had given her an echo of his anguish. She deserved better than that.

The vessel held the usual furnishings. From the refrigerator he took a bottle of champagne, opened it, poured two glasses to the brim.

'To you, my dear!' He lifted his glass in a toast. 'And to Jupiter and success!'

They drank and she refilled the glasses and sat beside him, smiling, happy in their intimacy.

'Talk to me,' she urged. 'I want to know you. Tell me about your early days.'

'The early days?' He shrugged and she knew the barrier he'd erected between that time and now would be left intact. 'When I was about eighteen I was, if nothing else, brash. Hungry to get on and make my mark like most other young men do. And I was as impatient as any. So I worked and did what had to be done and managed to accumulate a little wealth and then I had the biggest stroke of luck a man could have. I met Theodosius Zipadopolous. A genius.'

'Tell me about him.'

'I did. He was a genius. Now and again when they are needed they appear. Pasteur, Einstein, Newton, Faraday — those who change the course of events. Zipadopolous was one of them. A madman with a dream. He was fifty-three when I met him. An electronic wizard who built small devices intended for use in many, devious ways. I acted as his agent; arranging supplies, customers, deliveries, protection. Then, one night when he was drunk enough to be careless, he told me about his great secret. He told me about the drive.' He paused, remembering it, seeing again the workbench cluttered with components, the bones of their trade. Some phone-taps, false cash-machine cards, timers as small as a match, bugs, miniature recorders, tracers, electronic erasers, keys, triggers for supposedly secure data-banks. And the man himself, thin, mouth fringed with a straggle of hair, eyes like illuminated windows. 'At first I didn't believe him. Later I did.'

'And backed him?'

'Not exactly. I had some money but it wasn't anywhere near enough to provide what was needed. So I used what I had together with what I could persuade others to donate to get credit so as to enable Zipadopolous to concentrate on building a working model. It wasn't easy. It took a long time and at the end of it Theo had only months to live. Cancer — he was rotten with it. But he lived long enough to see his invention work.'

'The zipdrive,' she said. 'Of course! You named it after him.'

'No, that was a happy coincidence. He called it the zero inertial pulsator. The original papers bear that title but within a few months everyone was calling it what they do now.' He looked at his glass and drank and added, bitterly, 'Theo gave the world what it needed most at a time when it faced destruction. Bush-wars trembling on the edge of atomic conflicts. The Middle East, India, South America. The Guatemalian conflict showed how close we'd come to mutual wipeout. Then the zipdrive and the planets to stretch in. Pressures relieved and new industries revitalizing the economy. Yet who remembers Theodosius Zipadopolous?'

The man and the hard years, the crimes committed, the deals made, the contracts broken. Theo had lived on the fringe and those dwelling close had scented easy pickings. Others had tried to move in and, always, had been the never-ending need for money. Shamarre had provided it when things looked darkest; her dowry had finalized success, His first wife, the son she had born him — targets for those who had wanted him dead.

Beside him Lynne said, 'So that's how you got your fortune. You must be one of the richest men in the system.'

'That's not how it works.' Feyman poured himself more champagne. 'Those who chipped in cash wanted their cut. Others moved in to steal the patents once the drive had been proved viable. Big money tried to take over and other money, not so big but more vicious, wanted to muscle in. If a monopoly could have been established — but that was impossible. The thing was too big. It would have been like trying to tie down steam power or electric power or aviation. So I did the best I could and was satisfied with what I got.' And had used that money to make more. 'Enough of that. History can be a bore.'

'How can you say that?' She was fierce in her protests. 'The past is the ladder on which we climb to the future. Surely you can see that? Steam, electricity, atomic power — all steps upward. All victories. Ships and trains and planes and now space flight — what's next? The biggest step of all? On and out to the stars?' She looked through the port at the glowing splendor of the galaxy. 'We could almost reach them now,' she whispered. 'Almost.'

But almost wasn't good enough. At a twentieth the speed of light it would take eighty years for a vessel to reach Alpha Centauri. Almost as long to reach Proxima Centauri, the nearest star to the solar system. How to feed the crew during that time? Keep them supplied with water and air? Keep them alive? Keep them sane?

'We'll find a way,' she said when he reminded her of the difficulties. 'Men used to think they had to flap their arms in order to fly. They tried and died trying but others kept at it and learned that to fly you didn't have to emulate a bird. And we reached space when most people thought it was impossible. It was done with rockets and we had orbiting laboratories and settlements on the Moon before the zipdrive made it easy. Can you imagine what some of the original installations on Luna cost in terms of effort and finance? If we were willing to meet that price then we can pay it again. And we can't ignore the stars.'

They shone in her eyes, reflections from light that had streamed across the universe, illuminating her face and giving it a strange, mystical quality.

'Look at them, Max. Look at them.'

Suns scattered like jewels against the black velvet of infinity and around them circled worlds without number. Planets waiting to be developed or with alien life of their own all waiting to be reached and explored and harvested of their riches. Feyman narrowed his eyes against the brightness. It was hard to realize that what they saw was mostly illusion; a picture maintained by the persistence of vision. Flashes of brilliance interspersed with — what? Each pulse of the zipdrive took them from the normal universe and, for all anyone knew, threw them into regions of horror.

He said, to lighten her mood, 'Zip to Rigel. Spend a weekend on Sirius. Take the honeymoon trip to the Magellan Clouds.'

'You're joking,' she said. 'But it'll happen and soon.'

'Of course.' The wine had gone flat and he rose and went to the refrigerator pausing with his hand on a fresh bottle. 'Champagne or whiskey?'

'Whiskey. With ice and ginger ale.' As she took the glass she said, 'I'm serious, Max. We're on a rollercoaster of technological achievement and it can't be stopped. Computers, silicon chips, the internet, cyber space, rapid dissemination of news and availability. It took a long time to move from muscle power to steam. Not so long to move from steam to electricity. Less to reach atomic power. The zipdrive's been around for a quarter of a century now. If the trend continues we'll be reaching for the stars within a decade.'

'We're already reaching.' Feyman looked

at his drink then at her. 'They call it zipping the sun.'

'I don't get it.'

'If they can manage to do that they'll have improved the drive enough to try heading out. Some do it for kicks but all want the publicity.' He sipped and said, 'Will you be out there when the time comes?'

'Maybe — and you?'

'If we part it'll be your decision.'

'Max!' She stepped forwards him, one hand lifting to caress his cheek. 'Max, you — '

The buzz of the intercom interrupted what she was going to say. It was the captain with a message. They would land on Ganymede within the hour.

12

Ganymede was a torn and furrowed ball of stone some thirty-three hundred miles in diameter. A portion of it, facing Jupiter, was laced with underground tunnels and installations, blotched with domes and segmented runways, which ran between jagged peaks. A rough, tough place with a mining camp's air of urgency and bustle. The rest was as it had been since the beginning of time.

'Welcome to Ganymede.' Pietro Ludovice thrust out his hand, face illuminated with a smile as he greeted the new arrivals. 'A nice trip? Sorry about the landing delay but there's been a little trouble over at Beta 2. I've arranged for you to stay at the Golden Bucket.' His eyes moved towards Lynne. 'A suite. Is that satisfactory?'

Feyman nodded. 'Any news of Devin?'

'Nothing definite as yet. I got working on it as soon as I received your

163

instructions but the trouble with these dredgers is that they move around a lot. Devin worked for the Chi-Juscara Combine at one time then moved to the Helmond Corporation. Now, as far as I can learn, he's operating as a cowboy.'

'A freelance?' Lynne frowned. 'How did he manage to get a ship?'

'A dredge.' The agent smiled as he made the correction. 'We call them dredges.'

'Do they give them away?'

'Of course not, but there are ways; old vessels bought from the established companies as scrap and put back into service, others knocked up in small yards. Deathtraps mostly but the cowboys are always willing to take risks. Give them a hull, a zipdrive, a radio and air and they'll dredge the sun if the price is right.' He added, sourly, 'Most of them are subsidized by the big companies though no one will ever admit it. A form of blackleg labor and a cheap source of supply. A cowboy is paid by the load on delivery so will work his butt off to make it rich. The unions insist on limited operations, safeguards, regular inspections and all the rest of it. They're even talking of two-man crews.'

'Featherbedding?'

'What else?' Ludovice scowled his anger. 'Damned unions. They've fought computerization of the landing fields ever since the first dredge brought in the first load. We've managed to get some equipment in — even the unions could see it was murder to reject it — but with the increased demand it isn't enough. Anyway, now that Callisto is setting up as a receiving base they'll have to give way. You've luggage?'

Two cases which the agent loaded on the moving way, taking his place beside them once the others had been settled,

As they moved towards their hotel Feyman said, 'What about Devin?'

'He's one of the tough ones. He's been dredging for years and had more lives than a cat. Goes real deep — to grab the heavy stuff and takes chances which proves he's crazy. They're all crazy. It's a hell of a way to make a living.'

To zip across more than a half million

miles of space. To fall into the gaseous atmosphere of Jupiter and continue to fall until the layer was right. To open the hold and load with the selected vapor containing a devil's brew of seething chemical and mineral elements. To seal and zip up and out to where the giant containers waited to swallow the load. A pattern repeated over and over until the air ran low and the batteries needed recharging. Then to head back to the supply points and maybe take a rest and relax a little before facing death again.

And death was always close.

'They won't follow a set routine,' explained the agent. 'The big companies are forced to keep their men operating to a tight schedule but the damned cowboys are all over the place zipping in and out like maniacs. That's what caused the trouble over at Beta 2. They had ships stacked for landing and some nut jumped the queue. His air must have been low or something because the crazy bastard zipped out into the middle of the stack. God alone knows how many died. They're still searching the wreckage.'

Jupiter wouldn't have cared. The new bonanza, with its incredible wealth of gaseous elements now being ruthlessly plundered. Lynne looked at it through the curved transparency of the moving way. Its swollen bulk dominated the sky, the target of men riding mobile buckets. Even as she watched one came in to land; zipping out with a twinkle of identification lights. A squat, ugly shape with a tiny cabin and a grotesquely large hull. It looked like a monstrous insect; a queen gravid with eggs or a diseased wasp about to explode from accumulated gases.

She said, 'Why not use slave control?'

'Inefficient.' Pietro Ludovice picked up the cases as the moving way neared a junction marked with an illuminated sign. Stepping from the band he led the way down a sloping corridor flanked with safety doors and illuminated with fluorescent tubing. 'The radio-lag is too great. On average it takes about three seconds for a signal to cover the distance. Each way, of course, a total of six. So you see something on your screen, and it was there three seconds ago. By the time you correct it's another three. Add reaction time and there you are. Of course you get reaction time with a living pilot but you save the six seconds — and dredges aren't all that cheap.'

Dredges but not pilots — there would always be another wanting the chance to make his pile.

'And you can't use a slave when zipping,' reminded the agent. 'No radio contact is possible then. Of course we could operate from closer in, say Amalthea, but it's only a hundred miles in diameter. Europa's better but the Chernovsky-Saraya Russe operate from there.' He grunted as the corridor swept to the right to open into a rounded, flat-roofed area. 'Here we are. The Golden Bucket.'

It was a hotel buried in rock, a place of passages and lights, the roof at ground level and covered by a clear dome. Only the safety doors set at regular intervals made it different from any of the majority of hotels to be found on Earth. If an. accident breached the walls they would slam shut to limit the loss of air.

While Lynne was showering Feyman looked again at the photograph he had found in Moynihan's room. The message was brief; 'Come in — the water's fine.' Obviously the two men had known each other at one time but when and in what circumstance was still a mystery. Maybe Ludovice could discover a connection; the agent had left them at the suite to find Devin.

'Max?' Lynne came towards him, smelling of soap and freshness, dressed in nothing but a thin, red robe. 'Are we shocking your friend?'

'Ludovice? No.' The suite had two bedrooms as well as a lounge. 'What did you think of him?'

'Sharp, smart, eager to please.' Pausing she added, 'Greedy, too.'

'Which makes him normal for the territory.' Feyman flipped the photograph, the card which had been attached to it. 'What was Moynihan doing with this?'

She shrugged. 'Who knows? Maybe he found it somewhere or someone sent it to him.'

'Why?' As she hesitated Feyman said, 'Furneaux's son is a zombie. The boy is staying at the clinic in Eratosthenes. Your computer gave us Moynihan's name as someone who would have a cure. Or be able to supply one,' he amended as she frowned. 'Furneaux would be interested.'

'He'd waste his time with Moynihan. We know that.' Lynne took the photograph and card from his hand. 'Stop brooding, Max. Moynihan could have picked up the card anywhere. Someone could have dropped it in his shop. It can't be important.'

'Maybe you're right.' Feyman didn't think she was and he didn't trust coincidence but there was no point in pursuing the matter. 'There's nothing we can do until Devin is found. Get dressed and let's find out what Ganymede has to offer.'

It had it all.

Feyman halted at the entrance to the cavern beneath the Golden Bucket studying what he saw. The chamber was gouged from rock, decorated with drifting lights, hung with scented lanterns of a dozen hues. The floor was thick with gyrating dancers, harlots, panders, touts, parasites of every kind. The prey on which they battened were the men who stood or leaned at bar and table and gambling layout. Hard, tough, cynical men dressed in synthetic leathers adorned with a variety of sigils. Hard in ways other than brutality, tough in a different fashion than that of violence. They were dredgers, hard to themselves, tough to their feelings. Men who cared nothing for anyone or anything and the hardest and toughest were the cowboys.

'Drink!' yelled one. 'To Joe Ragin — may he hit the Layer!'

'To Ed Pierce,' shouted another. 'Dead and gone and somewhere smiling!'

'To Barney Hyme!' A man jumped on a table and lifted his glass. 'The best damned dredger there ever was or will be.'

'Like hell he was! What about Brad Murphy?'

'Good but not better.'

'Wanna prove it?' Another man jumped on a second table. 'Clear the deck! Bring the bottles!'

Containers that when smashed provided savage weapons; the necks sprouting a circle of brittle-pointed knives. Eager hands thrust a pair towards the contenders as others pushed the tables to within arm's reach. A few seconds and the area was clear, ringed with avid faces, the contenders left standing, weapons in hand.

'Fools!' Lynne shook her head as she watched from where she stood. 'They do this in the Belt. Why are men so stupid?'

A question that waited for an answer as the men swung into action. Glass smashed and splintered as they stabbed, parried, turned and twisted on the surface of the tables. To jump down was to admit defeat. To be forced from the limited area was to lose the victory.

A shout greeted the appearance of blood; a long gash beneath the left eye of the man championing the memory of Barney Hyme. More followed; from the knuckles of his opponent, a thin stream from beneath a tangle of hair, a flood from a slashed earlobe. The watchers yelled as, a foot slipping on blood, the challenger toppled to crash on the floor.

'To Barney Hyme!' The voices rose like thunder. 'The best!'

'The boys always like a little fun,' explained the waitress who served Feyman and Lynne after the commotion had died. 'They've a lot of tension to get rid of but they mean no real harm. Hungry?'

'Yes, but not starving.' Feyman reached for the menu, frowned as she retained it, 'Something wrong?'

'I figure you for a man who likes to take a chance now and again. Why not let me order for you? Fifty percent tip if you think I've hit the bell. Half price if I don't.' She was dressed in Edwardian style; long dress, bustle, high blouse and boots. A wide, black band circled her throat. Her hair, piled in an elaborate coiffure, was a work of art. Her painted face another. The effect was wantonly erotic. 'A deal?'

Lynne said, 'How could we refuse.' As the girl, smiling, moved away she said, 'Max, keep your eyes off that bitch.'

'Jealous?'

'Of you, yes.'

Flattery that amused him. As the meal, served with deft expertness, lived up to the waitress's promise.

As she served the after-coffee liqueur she said, 'Well, do I win?'

'You win.' Feyman added, 'You should be a psychologist.'

'I was, but I can earn more serving at table.' Her smile told him that was not all she did. The movement of her eyes towards his companion that she would have been more open had he been alone. 'Anything else I can do for you?'

'No!' Lynne was sharp.

'Yes.' Feyman overrode her. 'These dredgers. You must know them pretty well. Have you ever met a man called Devin?'

She frowned, thinking or pretending to. 'No, I can't say I have. Not that I remember. Not all of them come in here. The Blue Scoop over at Gamma 5 has quite a bunch of regulars. We share ours with the Bent Ladle. Devin, uh? Sorry.'

'Where else could I ask?'

'The business offices might know or you could try the brokers. If he's running

174

on his own the finance houses might give you a lead. Why not try the Ladle?'

It was like the Bucket; full of noise, lights, people. A man in gray stood close to the entrance arguing with a cowboy bright in a variety of sigils.

'Manfred, it's time you saw sense. The union offers you protection. You'll ride a decent dredge, have regular work, recognized pay, insurance, agreed bonuses. We're even working on sick pay and subsidized hospitalization. The others hold you in high regard — if you join they will follow.'

Manfred shook his head. 'No. I'm not interested.'

'But you're cutting your own throat.'

'That's not the way I see it.' Manfred lifted a hand and yelled to a painted girl standing beside a bar. 'Hold it, Myrna! I'm coming over!'

'Wait.' The union man caught his arm as the cowboy moved away. 'If you'd just listen — '

'No! You listen!' Manfred jerked his arm free and turned to scowl at the other. 'If I'd wanted it safe I'd have stayed on

Earth. Here I'm my own man. I work when I like and as hard as I like and dredge as deep as I like. What I get I sell to the highest bidder. I can make twenty times what your union men make. You want me to give all that up? Ride a dredge to orders? Punch a clock? Live like a machine? To hell with it.'

He stormed away to join the waiting girl, the union man frowning as Feyman touched his shoulder.

'You heard him?' he asked bitterly. 'What can you do with a nut like that?'

There were answers but Feyman liked none of them. A man should have the right to go his own way and if it was to hell in a bucket then that was still his prerogative. A point of view the union man wouldn't have agreed with and Feyman didn't mention.

Instead he said, 'You've a tough job. I guess some are harder to convince than others. 'Have you ever tried to sign up Devin? Arnold Devin?'

The union man looked at Feyman, his face, his clothes.

'You company?'

'No. I'm just looking for Devin. He's a cowboy. They say he could be anywhere.'

'That's the truth.' The union man shrugged. 'I've met him, I think. Months ago now. Tall, thin, wild-eyed, nose like a beak?' As Feyman made no comment the man said, 'Well, names change. The one I'm thinking of talked about dredging deep and running loads to Callisto. Maybe you'll find him there.'

13

The place was a copy of Ganymede; a little smaller, further out from Jupiter, but made of the same rock and with the same harsh aspect. The receiving site was cruder and the underground installations showed the speed with which they had been constructed. There were no moving ways.

'I'm sorry, sir.' Pietro Ludovice was apologetic as he walked at Feyman's side. 'I was certain. Devin had to be dredging from Europa but getting information from the Chernovsky-Saraya-Russe isn't easy. I'd sent queries here to Callisto but they're slow in replying.'

And the agent hadn't been given much time for the search. A fact he didn't mention but one Feyman bore in mind as he strode through junction and into another corridor. The green line he had been told to follow separated from others of different color to run like a narrow lawn before him. One that ended at a door. As he pushed through it a man rose from his desk his hand extended in greeting.

'Sir, this is a pleasure.' Major Hebron wore a uniform of dull brown marked with scarlet insignia. A high-ranking administrator of the combine that owned and operated the recently fabricated base on Callisto. One run as a commune with strictly regulated functions and an almost military discipline. 'Please take a chair. You would like some refreshment? Tea? Coffee? Something stronger?'

'I'd appreciate your help in gaining some information.'

'Of course. I understand the position.' Hebron smiled and nodded to Ludovice. 'It's good to see you again so soon, Pietro. I trust the arrangement as to the reciprocal air-charge has met with approval?'

'I anticipate no difficulty, Major.'

'I understand. These things take time. An economy measure,' Hebron explained to Feyman. 'If nothing else it will eliminate endless cross-accounting. You

179

see we do our best to be efficient.' A pause then he said, with blunt directness, 'I understand that you are interested in participating in our venture here.' Bait offered by Ludovice to grease the wheels.

Feyman said, with equal bluntness, 'I'm not interested in charity. Any participation I may make must be based on the possibility of a healthy return. My accountants will check your figures.'

'Those available to the public,' said Ludovice quickly. 'I've assured the Major of your discretion, sir. This operation has greater potential than a superficial examination would show.'

'You're dredging Jupiter. All right, you might be more efficient in terms of operating personnel and outing expenses but its still a matter of straight competition.' Feyman spoke directly to the officer. 'We're talking of millions here, maybe billions. I'll have to be sure the investment is sound. Just what do you have the other outfits lack?'

'I — ' Hebron broke off, looking at Feyman, reading his eyes, his face. 'In confidence?'

'Of course.'

'We're evolving a new technique. Deep-dredging. Ships will go down to the liquid layers and return loaded with pure elements. I shouldn't have to explain how high the profit-margin will be.'

Or how high the death rate. No wonder the combine was willing to use the services of such cowboys who were willing to risk their necks.

Things he didn't mention. Instead Feyman pursed his lips and nodded as if satisfied. Beside him Ludovice cleared his throat.

'There is another matter, Major. Devin? Arnold Devin? I contacted you about him.'

'Ah, yes, the dredger.' Papers rustled as Hebron searched his desk. 'Let me see, now. Yes, we have done business with him. The usual basis — we buy what he cares to deliver. His last load was received — ' he squinted at the paper, ' — a week ago.'

Feyman said, 'Does he reside here?'

'At times. For the past month almost regularly as far as we can determine.' He added, 'The type of man Devin represents does not conform to a desired pattern. He stays, he goes, he appears as and when he chooses. But he does have a cubicle on the eleventh level, decant nine.'

'Is he here now?'

'He could be. If not in his cubicle or the recreation area then in the repair yard or the hospital. We are proud of our hospital. Patients come from all over the Jovian System for treatment and care. Those suffering from various infections, broken bones, wounds — the recent accident at Beta 2 on Ganymede almost filled a ward. And, of course, there are the zombies.'

They were held in a room at the end of a passage and Feyman felt the sick, familiar chill as he looked at their blank faces, their dead, empty eyes. A cluster of things more disturbing than corpses for death was a natural part of the order of things. But what they had become was inexplicable.

'They come from all over.' The doctor in attendance was eager to be helpful.

'Ganymede, Io, Europa — the whole system. Some are returned to their families. Others are supported by their friends. The rest depend on the goodwill of those interested in their welfare.'

'Have you any idea what causes this condition?'

'No. There is no seeming correlation. They are of all types and both sexes.' The doctor illustrated with a wave of his hand. 'Zombiism strikes without warning. Mary Tiller was affected while washing a shirt. Brad Marvin while repairing an electrical fitting. Quentin Howard was found in a passage and Lucy Pattison slumped in her partner's arms while they were dancing.'

'The others?'

The doctor shrugged. 'Who knows what happened to trigger their condition? They were fetched here by friends or workmates. Some were sent by their employers willing to meet the costs. Our charges are not prohibitive.'

A man could watch a dozen as easily as one — the more so when they sat or lay sprawled on a plastic floor. All wore nothing but a short smock. Washing could be done with hoses. Food would be fortified slop from a bowl. Expediency dictated by expense; those on Callisto were not unkind but necessity determined their conduct.

'I'd like full details of every case,' said Feyman. 'Exact times, locations, situations, associations; all the data available.' Lynne had remained on Ganymede but she could incorporate the new findings into an updated program. 'Arnold Devin isn't here, of course. Would you know if he'd been a victim?'

'Not necessarily.'

'Aren't they all bought here? You claimed as much.'

'With reason, but not all are found. That is why it's impossible to say just how many have been affected. If a dredger zombies while working we simply never hear from him again. But we can't assume that all who vanish have been affected. Sometimes people zombie when alone. A man was found only last week. Jud Ivan, dead in his suit. He could have collapsed from a heart attack or he could have zombied and fallen. Others could be lying out on the rock and we'd never know it. Prospectors tend to be secretive about their movements.'

Men as stubbornly individualistic as the cowboys. Feyman remembered what Moynihan had told him about Franz Heinman. A connection? It would be something more for Lynne to work on.

'The man in the suit, Ivan? Do you know what model it was? The make?'

'I can find out. Shall I put the data with the rest?'

'Please. Is there anyone here who knew Devin well? A close friend? A woman? Anyone?'

Her name was Tara Riancon, a woman with short blonde hair and faded blue eyes. Life had made her hard, suspicious, and she looked at Feyman with wary caution.

'Arnold Devin? So I know him. So what?'

'Can we talk?'

'Am I stopping you?'

Feyman looked at the cubicle that was her home. A box gouged in rock containing a narrow bed, a chair, a small table, a thumb-locked cabinet. A bucket stood beneath the table. A jug held water. Against it an Earth-type prison cell was luxury.

'If you want the head it's down the passage.' A jerk of her head signaled direction. 'Showers the same. You pay for the showers. You pay for every damned thing in this place.'

'Does Devin live with you?'

'In here? That's a joke. He hired a box lower down.'

'Hired?'

'The rent ran out two days ago.' She sniffed and fumbled in the pocket of her faded blue smock. It yielded a small metal box touched with red and gold paint. Opened it revealed a thick dusting of white powder. She knocked the box to make a small pile, lifted it with her finger and thumb, sniffed it up her nostrils. Meeting Feyman's eyes she said, 'I'm low or I'd offer you a boost.'

'Cocaine?'

'You can buy it at the pharmacy. Most of the boys use it. It helps to clear the head and gives a lift. When they head out to dredge they need all the help they can get.'

The box closed with a snap. 'Sometimes it isn't enough.'

'Devin?'

'Maybe.' She shivered and looked distastefully at the cubicle. 'Let's get the hell out of here.'

The door had a thumb-lock to match that on the cabinet. It closed with a snap behind them and the woman led the way down the passage to an open area set with tables, chairs, loungers. A bar ran against one wall. A food-dispenser sold a variety of foods and soft drinks. Amusement and vending machines lined the space between openings. A poverty-copy of the Golden Bucket or the Bent Ladle.

She said, 'Hungry?'

'I could use something. A slice of pie.' Feyman handed her money. 'Get whatever you fancy.'

He looked for a table as she went to the counter, selected items, fed them into a microwave oven to heat. Pie for him and steak with all the trimmings for her. Wine accompanied the meal together with

187

coffee and brandy. If there was change she didn't offer it.

'I was crazy to come here,' she said. 'I could have made out in the Belt or on Ganymede but I fell for the publicity. Work for the combine, build your shares, wait for the jackpot. I never got off the ground.'

Feyman said nothing, waiting.

'Look at them.' She gestured at those wearing the dull brown uniforms. 'The elite. They work for points that grow to be converted to shares. The more you own the higher you rise. Me? I just work for pay and it's damned poor at that. What with rent for the cubicle, the cost of food, compulsory insurance, clothes, facilities — hell, they've got you each and every way it comes. I'd run but I need cash for zipfare. Arnold was going to supply it. We were both going to live high on the hog. One big dredge and he'd have it made.' She reached again for the small, metal box. 'Dreams,' she said bitterly. 'It's all goddamn dreams.'

'You can't be sure he's dead.'

'I'm sure.'

'How?'

'If he wasn't he'd be with me. We were close and he wouldn't just leave me to sweat. We'd made plans and — '

She broke off, fumbling with the small metal box, snuffing the last of the powder. 'He's hit the Eye.'

'What?'

'Dredger-talk. Hitting the layer is to strike it rich. Hitting the Eye — ' Her gesture completed the sentence, the edge of one hand slicing across her throat. 'The crazy bastard, I warned him but he wouldn't listen. He had it all worked out, he said. The dredge planned every inch of the way. Nothing could go wrong.' Her laughter was brittle. 'God! The times I've heard that!'

Feyman rose, crossed to a dispenser, paid for brandy, which he set on the table before her. Plastic cups served to hold it.

'Tell me about him,' he urged. 'The big dredge he was going to make — liquids?'

'How did you know?'

'I guessed.' There was no need to mention Hebron and what the major had hinted. 'How did he hope to get away

189

with it? Zip too low and he'd be in near-solid matter. A wipeout. Ride too long and the pressure would crash his hull.' If the storms didn't get him or unsuspected vortexes or stray fields of intense electronic energy didn't rip his vessel apart. 'He'd worked it all out, you say?'

'That's right.' She gulped at the brandy. 'He had it all set down in a book. Lists of numbers. He'd work over them for hours. It all depended on a pattern of routes as far as I could make out. Zip here, there, all over. A zigzag route — or maybe he was conning me. Once he said the secret would make him the fattest cat outside the Belt.'

A common boast among the dredgers when they were high on drink or drugs but, maybe, Devin had held more reason than most. Certainly he had been something special or why had the computer given his name? Devin and Moynihan. A dredger and a drunk — what could they have had in common?

Feyman said, urgently, 'Are you certain that he is dead?'

190

'Arnold? Sure. He has to be. I've been waiting and he hasn't come. I've asked around and he hasn't been seen, and they've stripped his cubicle. Taken all he owned. They wouldn't have done that unless they were sure he wouldn't come back.'

'Stripped his room? Who?'

'Magruder,' she said. 'The supervisor of the seventh on decant nine.'

He was small, furtive with eyes that moved in constant appraisal. One who held the master key that overrode the registered thumbprint-restriction on the locks.

'Devin,' he said. 'Arnold Devin. That's right. He went on a dredge and didn't come back so we assumed he died. We waited until the rent had expired and stripped his room.'

'We?'

'The commune.'

'That means you. What happened to his things? His property, did you put it in store?' Feyman saw the betraying flicker of the eyes. 'What happened to it?'

'I — '

'You sold it. Right?' Feyman smiled and lowered his voice. 'I understand. A man has to get on and you can rely on my discretion. But I want to know who bought Devin's things. I'll give you five hundred for the name.'

Magruder hesitated. 'Just between you and me?'

'You have my word.'

'It was Furneaux. Jafek Furneaux.'

14

He was a man who in other times would have watched men burn for the safety of their souls. Not as tall as Feyman, older, his face aquiline, the eyes veiled beneath heavy brows. He came forward to greet them as they were ushered into the room, smiling, lifting his hands in greeting.

'Max! It has been a long time. And your companion?' His eyes rested on Lynne as Feyman made the introductions. 'Lynne Colman? The name is familiar. Didn't you do some work for a subsidiary of mine? The Lenz-Hartman Company. You were working on — ' He broke off, smiling, shaking his head. 'It slips my mind. Perhaps you will enlighten me?'

She said, flatly, 'If the firm is a subsidiary of yours the information is as close to you as your nearest computer terminal.'

'You are a shrewd woman.' Furneaux

smiled, teeth white against the olive of his skin. 'One who has no intention of being tricked into divulging private information. I like that. Coffee?'

It was thick, rich, sweet as honey and as black as jet. Lynne glanced around the room as she sipped. The place was grandiose, one wall dominated by a broad window which showed Jupiter in all its splendor. Below, toy-like in the distance, reared the domes and enclosures of Gamma 5.

'You like the view?' Furneaux had been watching her.

'It's magnificent.'

'I must confess to having yielded to a self-indulgent whim. The same effect could have been provided by electronic means but, somehow, projections are never wholly satisfying. They lack something, a sense of propinquity, perhaps, which lessens their impact. More coffee?'

'Thank you.' As he returned her cup Lynne said, 'You have a really lovely home.'

'Home?' Furneaux shook his head. 'This isn't my home. It's merely to provide accommodation while I'm on Ganymede. I have others. They are a convenience. Max, you agree?'

Feyman said, dryly, 'My tastes aren't as yours. Neither are my interests.'

'But at times they clash — the Ventaha Franchise, for example.'

'Which you gained by outbidding me.'

'As you won the Bar-Kochar development.' Furneaux paused then said, 'My condolences on what happened to your daughter.'

'And mine on what happened to your son. Saeed would be three years older than Celia, I believe.'

'Four.' Lynne saw Furneaux's hand close around his cup. 'We share a common sorrow.'

'And have a common need. What did you learn from Devin?'

'Who?'

'Arnold Devin. A dredger working from Callisto. I know you know of him. I also know you intended me to learn you were interested or the supervisor would never have dropped your name.'

'I fail to understand.'

'I see.' Feyman set down his cup and rose to his feet. 'Come on, Lynne. We've wasted enough time.'

'Max?'

'He wants to trade,' said Feyman. 'His son is a zombie but, by God, he wants to trade. How much, Jafek? Ten million for what you got from Devin? Twenty?'

'You — ' Furneaux rose in turn to stand, shaking with anger. 'How dare you!'

'Dare?' Feyman gestured at the window, the luxury of the chamber. 'Has it got to you, Jafek? Do you think because you own this and other conveniences that you're some kind of a king? Am I supposed to come crawling, begging your help? To hell with you. Lynne?' Then, as she remained seated, he said, harshly, 'Please yourself.'

'Max! Wait!' She called as he turned towards the door. 'Don't be a fool, man. Sit down. You too!' She glared at Furneaux. 'Are you both such fools as to quarrel at a time like this? You're both looking for the same thing. Why not help each other to find it? Do you hate each other that much? Love your children so little?' Then, directly to Jafek, she said, 'The answer could be in Devin's things. Let's see if we can find it.'

The stuff was what she might have expected; a collection of trifles that represented the sum total of a human life. Jafek stood beside her as she stood before the table on which they had been spread. Feyman, to one side, watched as she touched, moved, touched again.

To Furneaux he said, 'What made you interested in Devin anyway? Did Moynihan give you a lead?'

'I did not see him.'

'Personally, no, but your agent did. Was the card he left another invitation for me to call on you?'

Lynne said, as Furneaux remained silent, 'At least tell us how you knew about him. About Devin too. Why make a mystery of it?'

'Caution,' he said. 'Habit, but it is really very simple. You have worked in the Belt and must be aware of the concern about zombies. Before Saeed was affected I had already instigated a program of research into the subject. One I intensified when I had a personal interest. And, while you may be one of the best retrievalists in the field there are others who know how to use computers.'

Some of which could be bribed to use their skills to raid private data banks in ways she had used herself in the past. They could have gained access to the initial stages if clever but she had taken certain precautions in the later sequences. Tagholm's name had appeared only after she had made the final search and it was possible Furneaux lacked the information. That or he was keeping it secret for reasons of his own.

'Moynihan and Devin,' she said. 'It seems we asked the same questions and came up with the same answers. We could also have made the same mistakes.'

Furneaux nodded. 'That is possible.'

'In which case we are all wasting our time.'

'That, also, is possible, but I don't think so. You asked what my agent had learned from Moynihan. It was very little. He met Devin when helping to rescue Franz Heinman. The man who had zombied on the Moon. Devin was in his party and he and Moynihan grew close for a while. They could have kept in touch.'

'Which accounted for the photograph,' Feyman said. 'Moynihan was connected with the Guatemalian fringe-war. He found a man who had zombied while wearing a suit. The doctor on Callisto told me of a similar case. A connection?'

'Lynne?'

She shrugged as Jafek put the question. 'It has to be simple coincidence. Two cases of men affected while wearing suits against how many others?'

'More than is generally supposed,' Furneaux was grim. 'The Belt seems to have a particularly high incidence but that may be because all cases are obvious. Others would have been buried beneath a blanket of wrong diagnosis. Not that it matters now. We have recognized the problem. Now we must find a cure.' He gestured at the litter spread on the table. 'Does that help?'

She had scanned it quickly, now she examined it again, carefully, taking her time. A creased and faded document opened to reveal a diploma issued by a school of natural medicine dated twenty-three years earlier. Some photographs all but one of women. She placed it down face uppermost and it watched her with wide and innocent eyes. Devin when he was young. He wore the cap and insignia of a UN volunteer. The badge was that of a staff entwined with snakes.

'The caduceus.' Feyman touched it. 'Our friend seems to have been interested in medicine.'

One that had quickly died, or one that he had been unable to pursue. A small book held close-set columns of type — an almanac of the Jovian satellites. Another listed elements to be found within the atmosphere of the gaseous giant and at what depth beneath the established but arbitrary air-space line. A bracelet held some battered charms. A folder a thin sheaf of papers containing certificates of navigational and operational efficiency. A pay-book listing charges due and install-ments paid on a dredge. A credit-book with a low balance. A few clothes, some small ornaments, a few books — one of poetry another of anatomy. As she moved them one slipped to the floor. Her eyes narrowed as she scanned the columns of hand-printed figures.

'It's a personal log,' said Furneaux. 'It seems to be nothing more than a record of his working life. The runs he made, their times, duration, loads, distances, direction, payment received. He must have been a methodical man.' As she continued to study the book he added, 'You seem to find more in it than I did. What have I missed?'

'Nothing.' She closed the volume with a snap. 'It's just what you said it was but I'm trying to fit it all together. There has to be a pattern somewhere. Devin, Moynihan — what do you think, Max?'

'I'm too tired to think.' Feyman yawned. 'Jafek, could I use your bathroom?'

'Of course.'

'And some coffee with brandy? American coffee, not Turkish?'

'It will be ready when you are.'

'Thanks.'

As he left Furneaux turned to Lynne

and said flatly, 'Are you his mistress?'

'Does it matter if I am?'

'If you are he is fortunate. I could envy him.'

'That would be better than hating him.'

'What?' His tone echoed his amazement. 'Why should you say a thing like that? Why should you even think it?'

'A feeling.' She rippled the pages of the book. 'The way you acted when we first met as if you faced an enemy. Your caution and reluctance to help.'

'One he shares.'

'No. He came to you,' she reminded. 'Maybe he thinks more of his daughter than his pride. Can you say the same about your son?'

'You wrong me! I — ' He broke off, fighting for control. 'Will you give me a straight answer if I ask you a question?'

'If I can, yes.'

'If Max finds the cure how can I be certain he will share it with me? You realize the power it would give him? If he had it there is nothing he could not demand. To me Saeed means more than life itself. I must be sure he is given the cure if it is found.'

'He'll get it.'

'But — '

'You're afraid. Both of you. You each thinks the other will bleed you dry if given the chance. My God! Is this what money can do to a man?'

'Please!'

'You'll get the cure,' she promised. 'You and every other poor bastard who has anyone gone zombie. And every zombie in the entire damned system. They'll get it if I have to steal it. Satisfied?'

He said, quietly, 'You shame me, but understand a father's concern. And yet you are right — money does warp the nature of a man. At first he wants it because it is the key to so much. Then it becomes an end in itself. A stupidity — after a certain amount the zeros cease to have meaning. And when you are faced with the reality that not all the money ever made can buy you the thing you want most then, if you are wise, you become humble. You learn to beg. To pray.'

'And — to give.' Lynne lifted the book

she held. 'To share. We can have copies?'

They were ready when Feyman rejoined them. He had showered, shaved, smelling of toilet water and talcum. He glanced at the copies Lynne held; one of the hand-printed book, others of the certificates and diplomas. Adding a generous measure of brandy to his coffee he sipped and nodded his appreciation.

'That's better. You've a fine bathroom, Jafek. Is the water recycled?'

Of course, but more is zipped in from Saturn. There's a sizeable reservoir held in a natural hollow back of the hills.'

'Which you own?'

'In which I have an interest.'

'Of course.' Feyman finished his coffee. 'We'd best be on our way. One last question, Jafek. Why did you place your son in the clinic at Eratosthenes? Do you think Anholt can find a cure?'

'He offers nothing but promises. Yet any hope is better than none. Why do you keep Celia in isolation? Surely she would gain by being in the company of her own kind?'

'I doubt it.' Feyman added, dryly, 'I've

never yet heard of an alcoholic who was cured by being kept in the company of drunks. Or of obesity being cured by putting the patient among a bunch of fatties in a kitchen. Like tends to breed like. And never forget that mental sickness can be contagious.'

'Saeed is not insane!'

'Neither is Celia. But can we be certain of the rest? As things stand it's convenient to call people zombies who aren't that at all. Anholt needn't be too particular who he takes into his clinic.'

Outside, on their way back to the Golden Bucket, Lynne said, 'That was unfair.'

'What?'

'You threw doubt on Anholt's integrity. Now Jafek will be worried.'

'Good.'

'It was deliberate?'

'Of course. What did you learn while I was away?'

'Did you deliberately leave us alone?' She read the admission in his eyes. 'I was right the first time we met,' she said bitterly. 'You've the makings of a first-class bastard. Jafek has reason to be wary of you.'

'And I of him. Did he ask you to steal the cure if and when we find it?'

'Not exactly.'

'What does that mean?'

'He was worried you wouldn't share it. He seemed to think you'd hold him to ransom.' Pausing she added, 'Was he right?'

Feyman said, 'Anholt broached Wolfe on the same matter and we know Anholt and Furneaux have something in common. Wolfe was wise enough to report it. I hope you've been honest with me.'

'If you mistrust me I'll quit now!'

'No,' he said. 'You won't quit. You'll come with me to Mars.'

15

The girl at the hotel information desk was a true Martian, twenty years old, native born, tall, slim, intriguingly shaped. Long, russet hair cascaded from a rounded skull to frame a piquant face bright with metallic cosmetics.

'Tagholm? Lars Tagholm? Are you sure he's a resident of Miliacus?'

Lynne said, 'No, we aren't certain, but this is the latest address we have.'

'Would you know if he is a citizen?'

'Of Mars? No. Would it make a difference?'

'A citizen has a world air-card which gives him the right to free access to all but private enclosures. A reciprocal agreement between the various zones,' she explained. 'A tally is kept in order to determine and allocate air-tax funds. I can check the data banks, of course, but it will take time.'

'Do the best you can.' Feyman's smile

was winning. 'I'm residing in the hotel — the desk will give you my room number. Feyman. Max Feyman. You'll find me grateful.'

'I'll do my very best, sir.'

'You've made a conquest,' said Lynne as they moved from the desk. 'Charm and money makes an irresistible combination.' She touched her hair as they passed a mirror. 'I look a mess. Would you object if I prettied up in your time?'

'Go ahead.'

He watched as she walked away with her graceful, long-legged stride. A woman displaying her charms and conscious of a rival. A childish reaction and, impatiently, he headed for the bar.

'Hello there!' A girl smiled at him. A Martian, almost a twin of the girl at the information desk. 'New to the planet?'

'Not exactly.'

'To Miliacus, then. The city of joy. Let me be the first to introduce you to a Martian speciality. Room 6757. In five minutes?'

'No thank you.' There was no reason not to be other than polite. 'But I appreciate you making me the offer.'

She returned the smile and moved away to accost another arrival. Feyman moved to the bar and ordered a fizzy drink served with lemon and ice. Sipping it he listened to the tired voice of a courier explaining, obviously not for the first time, some of the facts of Martian living to his charges, a couple of middle-aged matrons on their first visit.

'We can't zip, Sybil. It's quicker to go by crawler.'

'It's over two hundred metres! Why can't we go by ship?'

'I've told you — it would take too long, cost too much and isn't allowed. Look,' he punched the fist of one hand into the palm of the other. 'Let's get it straight. To get there by ship we'd have to zip up, wait for the planet to rotate, then zip down. But it's a restricted area so we'd have to come down a ways off and send for a crawler.'

'Why? Back on Earth — '

'This isn't Earth, Martha. For Christ's sake! How often — ' He broke off, swallowing. 'This isn't Earth,' he said again, patiently. 'And it isn't like the Moon. Mars has an atmosphere, not much, but enough to make things difficult. On the Moon you can zipout close to a dome and no harm's done. No shock-wave, you understand? On Earth it doesn't matter because people don't live under plastic. On Mars if you zipout too close to an installation you can rupture a dome and that isn't very healthy for those living inside. They can't breath the air but it's enough to carry the shock-wave. See? So we'll go by crawler. You'll like it. The scenery is magnificent and we might even be able to spot some of the damage done by the last storm. I hope you've both got strong stomachs?' He paused and looked from one to the other. 'Bodies, you know. People caught and mummified by the dryness and the sand. But if you don't want to see anything like that, television entertainment is provided.'

And would be ignored as they craned to see what probably existed only in the courier's imagination. Feyman finished his drink and was about to order another when his name came over the speakers.

The girl at information looked up, smiling, as he approached.

'That information you wanted, sir. I used priority as I knew you were in a hurry. I called your room but received no reply so I had you paged. I trust there is no objection?'

'None. What did you find?'

'Lars Tagholm isn't here at Miliacus. As far as I can determine he left some time ago. There are others with the same surname and it took a while to check — I explained how citizens often move around. They should register their new locations but many don't bother.'

'So?'

The girl had worked hard and received her promised reward. Lynne blinked from the screen of the phone he'd used to call her. She was in the sauna, hair glistening with moisture, sweat dewing her face, throat and naked shoulders. The lower edge of the screen masked the full swell of her breasts.

'Max! Did you locate Tagholm?'

'No, but I've a lead on someone who might know where he is. Jarl Keely over in

Syrtis Parva. I've arranged transportation.'

'Good. When do we leave?' Her eyes widened as he told her. 'In fifteen minutes? Max, that's ridiculous! Why not wait until tomorrow?'

He said, 'Parva is half-way round the planet. It'll be morning when we arrive.'

It was one filled with dust; grains caught by the wind and lifted from the desert to swirl in pluming devils of grit which fogged the thin air and piled against the taut plastic of domes and covered ways. A threat with its accumulated weight; one fought with gangs of men and blasts from gusting fans. A worrying time for those who had to live through it and Feyman could sense the strain as he led the way from the landing area to the hotel. That, at least, was secure with its walls of fused sand and windows of thick, triple-paned transparencies. The scouring dust might ruin the view and hamper surface activity but life continued via the mesh of tunnels and the sand, even as it accumulated, provided a measure of added protection.

'A nuisance.' Jarl Keely lifted his glass of iced citrus juice and vodka. 'Storms always are. This is only the tail-end of a minor blow but I've seen them really bad. Before we got the satellites coordinated for complete weather forecasts a storm could hit without warning. People forget that when they bitch about taxes.' He took a swallow of his drink. 'Well, that's life.'

One he'd lived hard. He was broad, hard, his face blotched and reddened by masses of burst capillaries. His eyes were a pale hazel prominent in bulging lids. He spoke in a husky whisper from some old injury to his larynx. A man of fifty who looked sixty-five.

He had joined them for lunch and had eaten well. Now he leaned back and looked over the dining room, the pale eyes noting, checking, evaluating. A woman, caught staring at his clown-like visage, blushed and became very interested in her dessert. 'You can't blame her,' said Lynne. 'She's probably never seen a man who's breathed space before.'

'And you have?'

'In the Belt, yes.'

'I was on the Moon.' Keely looked at his glass. 'Near Copernicus — we had an idea of establishing a closed ecology living area. Fishbowls were popular at the time and some backers were looking for investments. We were to check and make a report. Well, it was all routine for a while then it happened. One second I was standing on a ledge and the next I was falling. It was my own fault; a rotten patch I should have tested out but hadn't. I tried to twist on the way down to save the helmet but the rope snagged me and all I could do was wait as the rock came towards me. When it hit the faceplate fractured.' He added, bleakly, 'I'll never forget the way it broke. All in slow motion like some damned nightmare.'

'And?'

'I was lucky. I managed to get a patch in place and so seal the suit. Then the others came and got me.' Keely drained his glass and Feyman signaled the waiter to bring another drink. 'Thanks. Now about this man you're looking for. I've done some asking around since getting your message but haven't much to report as yet. Tagholm isn't in Parva as far as I know but, if you can afford to wait, he'll return in his own good time.'

'Which is?'

'A few weeks, maybe. A few months. Of course there's always the chance he won't come back at all. They go out and sometimes are never seen again. But, if he lives, he should be back in a while.' Keely stared from one to the other, frowning. 'Didn't you know Tagholm's a moocher?'

'What?' Feyman masked his disappointment. Tagholm, his last hope, and the man was worse than a fool. One of the idiots who roamed the planet looking for traces of the ancient civilization they were convinced had existed before the advent of Man.

Madmen who ignored accepted evidence in their pursuit of a dream. 'I can't afford to wait. How quickly can we find him?'

'That depends.'

'On money?'

'No. I'm assuming you're willing to spend what's necessary but it's more than that. Moochers are peculiar. They imagine everyone is after them to steal anything they might find. So they lie as to where they're going and make detours and all the rest of it. After a while they don't even trust their own shadow. They establish emergency caches of supplies so as to stay out longer than anyone expects. They'll walk to other settlements and fail to register and even report themselves dead. They're crazy, the lot of them.' Paranoiacs, but they had good reason to be cautious.

If they did find what they were looking for it would bring instant fame and riches.

A single artifact could do it. A scrap of anything that would prove their case and each and everyone of them would kill to get it.

Lynne said, 'How do they manage to live?'

'They work when they have to' explained Keely. 'Like now. You'll find a few of them clearing sand. Sometimes they bring in things to sell; shops buy them for the tourists who want mementoes. They'll beg and lie and cheat and even steal if they think they can get away with it. Anything to raise a stake and, once they've got it, they're out again.' He looked at a window fogged by the recent storm. 'In weather like this a lot of them will stay out.'

To die, mummify, eventually to become a part of the sand that had killed them. Lynne hoped Tagholm wouldn't be one of them. Leaving Feyman making final arrangements with Keely she paused to wait beside a booth where a young couple were buying a souvenir. It was a piece of stone fretted into a delicate lace-like pattern by the action of dust and wind. A snowflake which caught the light and reflected it in a shimmer of rainbow hues. The price they finally paid was a high multiple of that given to the moocher who had found it.

She turned as Feyman joined her. He was silent in the elevator and she sensed his tension as they left the cage to head down the passage to their suite. Drinks had been provided as a part of the service and she moved to the tray, poured two drinks, handed him a glass.

As he took it she said, 'Max, I'm sorry.'

'For what? Another dead end?' Feyman swallowed half the drink at a gulp. Finishing it, he said, bitterly, 'Moynihan's a drunken artist hooked on dope. Devin was a deadbeat dredger. Tagholm's a nut. What the hell went wrong with that computer you used?'

'Nothing. It's one of the best and you know it.'

'Can you check your findings?'

'As soon as I gain access to a terminal. You want me to rerun the entire program?'

As he nodded she said, 'It will take time and do no good.'

'Why not? It's obvious the original answer must be wrong. There's no connection between the three men. No answer either. Could you have made a mistake?'

'No.'

Her flat denial triggered his anger. 'Why not, for God's sake? You're human, aren't you? Fallible?'

'And you're tired and disappointed and upset.' Her anger flared in turn. 'But don't take it out on me. I feel as badly about it as you do. You think I've let you down. I may not have found the right answer but I did my best. I checked and rechecked and incorporated systems designed to eliminate error. If I did it a thousand times over I'd still get the same result.'

'Even incorporating the new data?'

'Maybe. I don't know. I can't promise anything. I'm sorry.' She looked at her drink then slammed it down hard on the tray. 'What the hell am I apologizing for? You hired me to do a job and I did it. I never promised more than I delivered, but, for you, that wasn't enough. You wanted a miracle.'

And still wanted it.

Feyman said, coldly, 'You're not a hysterical woman so don't start acting like one. Displays of temper and hurt pride will get us nowhere. More impor- tant they won't help Celia. Can't you understand, woman, she is what this is all about!'

A harsh reminder and she remembered the girl, the other zombies she had seen.

'I'm sorry. I mean that. What do you want me to do?'

'Get to work on the computer. Can you add the new data to the program without having to run the entire thing?'

'An updated version? Yes, of course, I'll check with the facilities here and get on it right away.'

'There's a better method. Go to Earth. You can stay in the house at Pasadena — the computer there is ready for use.' He added, 'I'll radio Harman to have you met.'

Her departure left a void — he hadn't realized he would miss her so much. The ship he'd chartered had left within twenty minutes of making the decision and now would be nearing Earth. Time for him to have done what needed to be done but not for his tension to have eased. Always it was like this when he had to wait. To be forced to rely on others when his nature demanded that he be taking an active part.

A shower helped and he went to bed to lie staring at the ceiling. What had gone wrong? Why had the computer failed?

Would Lynne resent being sent to Earth? Change her feelings towards him? Maintain the cold hostility that had been present when they parted?

Questions that spun in his mind until his lids grew heavy and he slept.

To wake, hours later, to the demand of the phone.

From the screen Keely said, 'I could have found something. A friend of Tagholm's. You want to meet him?'

16

The storm had cleared with the coming of night and now outside the complex the domes rested beneath the chill light of the stars as if made of snow. An illusion; the water on Mars was scant and buried deep or locked in chemical combination with various minerals, but one strong enough to make tourists dream of the Mars of earlier times. A place of canals and verdant plains, of seasonal floods and shallow seas. The planet of legend where strange beasts vied with beautiful people and life was full of romance, excitement and adventure beneath the twin lights of racing moons.

A legend which Quan Ki Nor, Magus of the Sacred Order of the Scarlet Dawn, did his best to promulgate.

'He's known to the moochers,' explained Keely after Feyman had joined him in the bar of the hotel. 'They don't trust him, of course, but sometimes they get a little careless and he picks things up. He might know where Tagholm is to be found.' He glanced at his watch. 'I want to hit him at a ceremony. That way we can be sure of nailing him.'

The door to the home of the order was closed, decorated with abstract symbols, flooded with ruby light from a concealed source. It opened to Keely's knock and they passed into a vestibule guarded by an acolyte wearing a scarlet robe. Money changed hands and he opened an inner door. Beyond it the Magus was conducting a ceremony.

He wore a robe similar to that of the acolyte but made of some shimmering material heavy with flashing jewels. He carried a sword that glittered and his fingers were loaded with rings. The audience was composed of men and women of mixed ages but with a preponderance of old. Music came from a recorder and the fumes of incense rose in thick plumes from twin braziers. The walls of the chamber were daubed with mystic signs and articles of an esoteric nature rested on an altar-like slab of polished stone.

Feyman watched as the ritual progressed. It was neatly done, the gesticulations not over-emphasized, the chants conveying some basic truths though the terminology was loaded with bizarre associations. A form of announcement; a recitation of pseudo-history dealing with the distant past when giants had strode over the plains of Mars which had then been blessed. A Golden Age ended by war and tribulations and now lost to all but a handful of those who were masters of esoteric truths and mystic arts. To believe was all. To have faith. To maintain the respect due to the sages. To be young again. To follow the right path and discover the secret way.

In various forms he had heard it all before but now it held a greater impact. The incense that fogged the air could hold some mild hallucinogenic drug. The music held oriental connotations that hinted at the ripple of distant waters, the thin, sparkling chimes of wind-blown glass.

The Guru himself with his voice like an organ.

Feyman looked beyond the theatrical

garb and saw a man of advanced years, thin to the point of emaciation, the eyes wide-spaced, luminous. The mouth was a gash, the chin wreathed in a fuzz of silver hair. The hands were those of an artist.

The ceremony ended. The offering bowl was passed and returned heavily laden. The acolyte announced that those seeking further instruction into the greater mysteries should make their application in writing. He came forward when, all the others having left, only Keely and Feyman remained.

'The ceremony is over.'

'I know.' Keely was brusque. 'I want to see the Magus. Give him this.' He handed the acolyte a card. 'We've met before.'

Ten minutes later they were ushered into the inner sanctum.

Quan Ki Nor had changed. The scarlet robe hung on a peg, the sword was in its sheath, the rings had been stripped from the thin fingers. Now he wore a conservative costume of pants and blouse and soft, plastic shoes. A percolator steamed to one side of a table the aroma of coffee filling the air.

'Jarl Keely.' A thin hand rose in greeting. 'Max Feyman. I am honored You will join me in coffee.'

An order, not a request, the Magus pouring without waiting for an answer, handing out thin, porcelain cups. He lifted his own as if in a toast.

'To life, my friends, and to death. Those who come to me do so because they wish to hear of the things they long to believe. They want to know of the old and ancient race, which lived on this planet when it was green and fertile and still had to suffer the catastrophe that made it as it is now. The race which lives here still; dreaming in their secret vaults and waiting for the time when they will rise and resume their discarded power. The Sacred Order of the Scarlet Dawn is dedicated to serve them.'

He drank and, without changing tone, said, 'How can I help you?'

Feyman said, abruptly, 'You know why I'm here?'

'You search. You hope to find. One man seeking another. Do you intend him harm?'

'No. The reverse.'

'What do you want with him?'

'That's my business.' Feyman added, 'I want to talk to him. Ask him some questions. It's possible he can help me.'

'To buy that which money cannot obtain?' Quan Ki Nor smiled and lifted his hands, palms upward. 'What if Lars Tagholm cannot help?'

'I don't know.' Feyman felt his shoulders sag at the thought of it. Hope was dying but a stubborn fragment remained. Once it had gone — what then? 'But he won't have wasted his time. Can you tell me where he is? How to find him?'

'If I do?'

Keely said, 'I'll take care of that. You know you can trust me.'

'Yes, Jarl, I trust you.' Quan Ki Nor made an odd gesture with his right hand. 'Very well. You are familiar with the seventh decant? The third quadrant? There is a peak bearing an unusual form. You know it?'

'Yes. Eagle rock.'

'The shape of a bird. Follow the

direction of the beak. Now, for your ear alone.' The voice of the Magus fell to a whisper as he masked the thin-lipped mouth with his hand. As he straightened Quan Ki Nor said, 'You understand?'

'Yes.'

'We shall meet again.' The Magus repeated the odd gesture. 'May the ones now gone and sleeping extend to you their protection.'

Outside Keely said, 'The old man liked you. That's good. He hopes you like him too.'

'Money?' As the other nodded Feyman said, 'He'll get it after I've found Tagholm. You'll arrange things? We'll need transportation of some kind. A crawler or rocket plane and — ' Feyman saw Keely shake his head. 'What's the matter?'

'You're forgetting what I told you about moochers. They run at the sight of a crawler and what chance would you have of spotting a man from a plane if he doesn't want to be seen? The only way to reach Tagholm is on foot.'

'Maybe, but we don't have to walk

every step of the way. Get what you need and let me know when you're ready. I'll be in the hotel.'

In his suite Girard was waiting.

Feyman had sent for him after Lynne had left for Earth and the security man had wasted no time. He leaned back in a chair, a slim notebook balanced on his knee. The book was a part of his façade; Girard had a photographic memory and total recall. An attribute he chose not to advertise but which had helped to make him foremost in his profession.

He said, 'There was a call for you, sir. It's taped.'

He looked at his notebook as Feyman moved to the phone, adjusting the baffles to gain both aural and visual privacy.

The call was from Lynne Colman. She was smiling.

'Max, darling, I've been a fool. I had to call and let you know that. It was all my fault. I shouldn't have felt so badly about you ordering me back to Earth. You were right. I know you're worried and tired and I had to act like a prima-donna. Please forgive me, darling. I miss you so much. I'm doing as you asked. I hope you have luck with Tagholm and hope to see you soon. Goodbye for now, dearest, remember I love you. I love you!' Her lips pursed in a kiss. 'Think of me if you have the time.'

The voice and image died as the message ended. A taped recording of a taped call; the radio time lag between the planets was about five minutes now. A ten-minute gap between asking a question and getting an answer was tedious — it was better to zip and meet face to face.

'Sir?'

Girard was waiting and Feyman realized he'd been sitting and staring at the phone. The message had cheered him. At least it had removed one of his worries. Lynne had probably guessed how he'd felt and had done something about it. Odd how a direct statement of affection could boost a man's ego. Odder still why so few women were willing to cater for that need.

Rising he said, 'What's your assessment?'

Girard opened his notebook. Even

when in repose the man radiated the aura of a watchful tiger and it matched his basic nature. Amoral, self-sufficient, unhampered by obstructive ethics yet intelligent enough to recognize the necessity of abiding by a code that would gain him the things he wanted. A mercenary; true to his contract in order to enhance his reputation.

All wealthy men had someone like him.

He said, 'I put men to work as soon as I arrived. Quan Ki Nor came to Mars in the early days and has worked at several things including water-mining, construction, mapping and disposal. For the past eight years he has been the Magus of the Scarlet Dawn. There is a suspicion he is connected with unlawful activities but I'm waiting for evidence and confirmation.'

'Criminal activities?'

'Possibly. Many things on Mars aren't illegal as they are on Earth.'

Feyman said, impatiently, 'I know that. I'm talking about murder, mayhem, extortion. Has he any record?'

'No.'

'These suspicions — are they in the official files?'

'They are.' Girard didn't explain how he knew. 'He is most probably a fence and we know for certain he practices hypnotic therapy.'

'Which isn't a crime on Mars.'

'Admitted, but it throws a light on his character. I'd say he was a cunning entrepreneur.' Girard pretended to consult his notebook. 'Keely is what he seems to be. The incident on the Moon actually happened as he said it did. He came to Mars shortly afterward. He was probably conscious of his facial appearance. He has acted as a guide and has tried his hand at prospecting. He has a good reputation. His association with Quan Ki Nor began about four years ago.'

Feyman held out his hand. 'Does this mean anything to you?' He repeated the gesture the Magus had made. 'Again?'

'Please.' Girard watched it closely. 'It's a recognition signal of the Cham-Gouch. They were the early arrivals and swore mutual brotherhood and aid. I thought the society was extinct. Maybe Quan Ki

Nor hoped you would respond to it.'

Or had given a covert warning of what could happen if faith was betrayed. Had the signal been aimed at Keely? Why hadn't he admitted the long-standing association? What had been whispered in his ear?

The exact whereabouts of Tagholm?

Details of a secret plan?

Feyman said, 'About the present situation — what do you advise?'

'Extreme caution. On the face of it the matter could be as it seems but it could also be a trap. You are a wealthy man and an opportunist would recognize the advantages of holding you for ransom. We must guard against that possibility. I would suggest that you ask Keely to bring Tagholm to you here in Parva. I would also suggest you guard against an imposter.'

'You have some background?'

'A little and mostly from local sources. People know him. Fortunately he has only been a moocher for the past three years. Before that he was an engineer. He came to Mars about twenty years ago with his father who died in a storm shortly afterwards. He was involved with a group demanding free water and air rights for all citizens but dropped out to do some electronic research. He was quite good at it. You probably have his physical data but the time spent mooching could have altered his superficial appearance. Let's check the position given.'

Feyman went to the phone, called the desk, gave orders. Within minutes a page was at the door a rolled map in his hand. It was one of the designated area taken from an orbiting satellite. Detail was not as clear as it could have been due to extreme enlargement.

'Here.' His finger touched a point. 'Eagle Rock is a known landmark and I had them mark it for me. The beak points in this direction.' His finger traced a thin line heading towards the northwest. 'That's all I know.'

'Let's see if we can determine more.' Girard stooped over the map. 'Assuming transportation to the rook and following the line we come to a deep crevasse which runs for miles to either side of the route-line. Something before that? This, perhaps?' His finger touched a crater.

'Or here?' An inch on the map but miles on the surface. 'Or, of course, the men hired could be a part of the gang and you'd be taken as soon as you'd left the complex.' He straightened. 'Are you insisting on going, sir?'

'Yes.'

'Then we'll take what precautions we can. I'll have my own men watching; they can be disguised as moochers and scattered over the area. I'll place them before you leave.'

'No!' Feyman was emphatic. 'They would be spotted and I don't want to frighten Tagholm away. We'll set a ship in a synchronous orbit. You'll be standing by with another. I'll carry a radio-alarm. Something small. And a weapon of some kind.' Feyman paused, thinking. What other precautions to take against the unknown? 'I'll phone Keely and tell him we'll leave at midnight. That give you enough time?'

Girard said, 'Make it dawn, sir. You'll be easier to spot.'

17

They left an hour earlier, the crawler moving slowly through the darkness, headlights bathing the rocky ground ahead. Keely sat beside the driver. Feyman slumped in a chair behind together with a half-dozen others and bales of supplies. Too many supplies for so few men but he guessed Keely was playing it safe. Air, food and water together with sacs for personal and community use. Something that looked like coils of thin rope. Something else that could have been a stretcher.

Beside him the sealed window showed the eerie expanse of the Martian desert, silvered now with starlight, ghostly with dancing shadows created by their own illumination. The light in the cabin was subdued; a soft, pale blue that did little to harm night-vision, but the headlamps streamed rays of brilliance that were caught and reflected by the boulders and mounds of dust from the recent storm. Sand that rose from beneath the treads of the crawler and created a thin, transient fog that marked their passage.

Feyman sat, yielding to the fatigue that added comfort to the chair. It was tempting just to relax and let his imagination run wild. To dream of old and ancient cities moldering beneath the sand. Of palaces like lace with tinkling bells and warriors and maids of stunning beauty. Of elfin towers and bubbles of iridescence, of shimmering swords and the burning glitter of jewels.

Of Lynne and her face, smiling, wonderful . . .

'Max?' Keely was beside him, face concerned. 'Are you all right?'

Feyman blinked and straightened, aware that he had dozed. 'I must have fallen asleep. How are we making out?'

'Fair enough. The sand's slowing us down a little but nothing to worry about. We made a detour. I wanted to show you something. See?'

Feyman followed the pointing finger and saw a figment of his dream; frosted minarets, pagodas, pinnacles, spires and towers all glistening with a silver sheen. Syrtis Parva, coated with its own waste, plastic and buildings rimed with molecules of ice ejected by the vents and held by static electricity. A wedding cake of bizarre proportions which, suddenly, blazed with gold and ruby fire.

Dawn and, for a moment, Feyman was lost in a vision of resplendent glory. It died as the crawler lurched and the city fell from view.

'How far to the rock?'

'It'll take a while yet.' Keely squinted through the window. 'That's why I wanted to leave early. Dawn's busy time at the locks and we've avoided the rush.'

Avoided possible followers too and those who might have shown an unhealthy interest. As the headlights faded to a dull flood of luminescence Feyman said, 'How long is it going to take? The entire journey, I mean?'

'Another reason for starting early. With luck we'll be there by night.'

They were on the equator or as near as made no difference. A total of thirteen hours of daylight traveling time. Seven in the crawler would cover, at normal speed, about two hundred miles. Six on foot another twenty. Feyman thought of the map he had studied, recalling details and distances. The detour Keely had mentioned was a decoy to cover their real direction of travel; Eagle Rock was not more than a hundred and fifty miles from the city. Or were they heading for it at all?

Feyman said, keeping his voice low, 'Just where the hell are we going?'

'The rock. You heard Quan Ki Nor.'

'I didn't hear what he whispered in your ear. And we're heading too far east.'

'A detour. I told you about it. You don't need to worry.'

Feyman wasn't as certain but worrying now would serve no purpose and it was pointless to argue. He leaned back, relaxing, yielding to the hum of the engine, the undulating movement of the vehicle. Outside the day had brightened and he closed his eyes against the glare.

This time his sleep held no dreams and he woke stiff and numb to find they had halted in a narrow defile running between jagged peaks.

'Time to get out and walk.' Keely came towards him as Feyman rose and stretched. The others had already passed through the airlock aside from the driver who lounged in his seat studying a manual. 'He stays here,' Keely explained. 'Ready?'

The suit-drill was a familiar routine. As he landed on the ground beyond the airlock, snug in the security of his own environment, Feyman looked around. The day was old and he knew he had slept longer than he'd guessed. As he stamped the tingle of returning circulation from feet and legs Keely hooked him into circuit.

'Check?' His grunt answered Feyman's lifted hand. 'Let's go!'

The others had been briefed, Feyman guessed, certainly they knew what to do. Always someone was at his side to guide and support. Assistance he could have managed without but which he accepted without argument. The thing that looked like a stretcher traveled with them and he had no wish to be strapped down and carried.

Three hours later he would have welcomed it.

'You all right?' Keely came to join him, staring into his helmet, voice a rasp over the wire. 'Can you manage?'

'I'll manage.' Feyman hoped he wasn't lying. 'How much further?'

'A few miles. It gets easier as we go.'

They moved on over a nightmare of broken stone, crevasses, narrow passes, patches of slickness, slides, walls of eroded rock. Terrain that gradually smoothed into a pocked and toothed expanse, over which even a crawler would have trouble.

Feyman slumped as Keely ordered a rest, lying back to stare at the empty sky in which stars were beginning to shine. In an hour it would be night and the cold would move in to add to the hell.

The sacs would provide protection against it; the flexible bags into which they could crawl and seal the envelopes and eat and sleep like any moocher. Die like one if the membrane ruptured, the air failed, a storm rose to bury them in crushing sand.

Bleak thoughts and Feyman was glad when they resumed progress. Two miles further and he saw the light. Three and it became a lantern that died as they came close. It had marked a defile at the end of which was a door set in the side of a hill.

Feyman caught Keely by the arm. 'Tagholm?'

'Inside.'

In a room littered with equipment that gleamed in the harsh glare of suspended lights. One that threw Feyman back in time. Decades ago he had seen just such a place, just such items of scientific association on tables scored with work and stained with neglect. And Theo had sat as the man was sitting, leaning a little forward, the light making stained glass windows of his eyes.

But Theodorius Zipadopolous was long dead and the place he had worked in long reduced to scattered rubble. And where he had been tall Tagholm was slight but both had the same, fanatical light in their eyes.

'You all right?' Tagholm stared his concern. 'Is something wrong?'

'No.' Feyman shook his head to clear it from the illusion. 'You just reminded me of someone I used to know. Lars Tagholm? I'm Max Feyman.'

'I know.'

'Do you know why I'm here?' Feyman wasn't surprised at the other's nod; there had been time for investigations to be made and a message to be sent. 'I'll come right to the point — can you cure a zombie?'

Tagholm said, 'You're a very rich man. Do you think your money can work a miracle?'

'No.'

'You could be wrong. Sit down. Tired? You look pretty beat to me.' Tagholm dumped a bottle and glasses on a table. He waved at a chair. 'Sit down. Relax. You're not going anywhere.'

'I'm where I want to be.' Feyman sat and reached for the glass thrust towards him. Keely and the others had stayed outside or, more probably, had made their way to other quarters. If Tagholm

243

wanted to play games he had no choice but to ride along. 'But there must be easier ways of getting here. It's years since I did so much work in a suit.'

'Work?'

'Not for you, maybe, but I'm out of condition. Crossing that broken ground wasn't easy. A stroll for a moocher is more than most people can take.' He tasted the wine. It was red, strong, and he wondered if Tagholm hoped to get him drunk. 'What shall we drink to? Mars?'

'The Old Ones!'

The choice of toast was betraying. Feyman looked around as he lowered his glass. A laboratory of some kind and a secret one. In his experience such places went hand in hand with trouble.

'The Old Ones,' he said. 'What would they think if they were here now? Mars dead and empty — all they knew vanished without trace. Maybe it's better they stay away.'

'You think they have a choice?'

'Don't you?' Feyman poured more wine into the other's glass. Getting people drunk was a game two could play. 'Isn't that why Quan Ki Nor lets you use this place? He does, doesn't he?'

'It was a supply dump set up for the use of water-engineers years ago and abandoned soon after. Quan found it and fixed it up and moochers use it at times. If they're sick,' explained Tagholm. 'Or stranded. Or have broken equipment. It's a long way to Parva.'

'Longer to Niliacus. Why did you leave? Did you get tired of fools laughing at you? Didn't they understand the importance of your work?' He was guessing but he'd dealt with people like Tagholm before. Some things were obvious. 'There could be whiskey in the supplies. Brandy even. You want I should have Keely dig it out?'

'This'll do.' Tagholm reached for the bottle. 'So you've got a girl who zombied, eh? Too bad. Young? Pretty?'

'Yes to both.' Feyman fought to remain patient. The man would move in his own time. 'Have you ever seen a zombie?'

'Sure.'

'Here? Moochers?'

'No. If they zombied who the hell would know? It was when I was working with Victor Cruse over at Titarum Sinus. That's on the other hemisphere. He had a workshop and I used to help. Did you know I was an engineer? He had a theory as how to boost the zipdrive. You know how it works? The pulsing and all that? Victor figured that if you could cascade the pulse you'd get a geometrical increase in displacement. Get it?'

'Cascade, eh?'

'That's right. As things are we've got a twentieth light speed as makes no difference. Point zero five displacement velocity.' Tagholm blinked, the wine, finally, seemed to be getting to him. 'Victor figured that if you could pulse while displaced you'd add a multiple factor. Not double but twenty times as much.'

Light speed and, if you could do it again, twenty times that velocity. It would bring the stars within reach. Not a new dream but Feyman had never heard of Victor Cruse.

'He's a genius,' said Tagholm. 'Or, at least, he was. He was getting close to what he was after when it happened. One second he was bending over his test model and the next — 'Tagholm snapped his fingers. 'A zombie.'

'Just like that?'

'I damned near saw it happen. I was in the shop with him checking the readings. He was talking and I heard him break off. I turned and saw him bending over the model like I said. A zombie.' Tagholm drained the bottle. 'You want more? I'll get more. Why save it?' He delved in a cabinet and returned with a fresh supply. 'Here.' He slopped wine into the glasses. 'To Victor Cruse!'

He gulped as Feyman sipped. 'You said he was close. How close? Had he managed to cascade?'

'I'm not sure.' Tagholm rubbed at his cheeks. 'He didn't tell me the details but we talked a lot about displacement and where and how it took place and all that. The main trouble seemed to be harmonics. That's what he told me but he could have been lying. He didn't want anyone to snatch the discovery if he hit the jackpot.'

'Displacement?' Feyman pretended an

interest he didn't feel. Keep the man talking. Keep him drinking. Sooner or later he would let something slip. 'Did he think that was important?'

'Don't you? Haven't you ever wondered where the hell you go to when zipping? You don't stay in this universe, that's for sure, so where do you go? Victor figured there could be an alternate space-time continuum running beside our own. When we zip we duck into it and then out again.' He paused and looked into his glass. 'Maybe that's where they all went.'

'Who?'

'The Old Ones. Those who were here before us. On the world that became the asteroids too, maybe. Perhaps they had to leave when it blew all to hell and gone.'

Using miraculous powers and their vast knowledge which could tame the elements, eliminate distance, grant them eternal youth, immortality, vigor and vitality. But if they had been so smart where were they now?

A question Feyman didn't ask. Instead he said, 'So you worked for Victor Cruse.

When did he zombie?'

'Three months ago. Some people are taking care of him at Titarum Sinus. A religious order of some kind. I visit when I can.' Tagholm poured himself more wine. 'A genius,' he mourned. 'He had a plan all worked out to zip ice from Saturn and dump it on and around Venus.'

Feyman said, 'Why Venus? Why not use the effort to reclaim Mars?'

The trigger worked as he'd hoped.

'Mars!' Tagholm reared from his chair to stand, swaying, glass in hand. Lifting it he roared, 'To the Old Ones!'

Feyman joined the toast.

'You're a good man,' said Tagholm as he slumped back into his seat. 'A bastard in some ways but you believe and I'm going to help you. Your girl, eh? Your little girl.'

'Can you cure her?'

Smiling Tagholm said, 'I know who can.'

18

It had been a long night. Feyman turned, slowing as he felt the throb at his temples. The bunk was narrow, the mattress hard; things he hadn't noticed when Keely had helped him to bed. Tagholm had showed an unexpected capacity and had insisted on continuing the bout long into the night. Towards the end Keely had joined them.

'You awake, sir?' One of the porters was at his side, a mug of steaming coffee in his hand. If a criminal he was polite. 'Here, this could help.'

Feyman nodded his thanks and took the mug. It was hot and he blew on it before taking a cautious sip. The porter had used his imagination — the coffee was laced with brandy.

Putting it aside he glanced at his watch. He had been in the depot fifteen hours,

A long time — and what had he gained?

Tagholm was a fanatic and therefore dangerous. A man who could easily persuade himself that the end justified the means and if it took murder to accomplish his objective then murder would be done. Keely was different but loyalty withered when set against a fortune. Quan Ki Nor stood to gain and no matter what happened could hardly lose. The porters? Maybe they could be relied on and maybe not — but Feyman had his own defences.

The watch was more than it seemed. A twist and pressure on a stud and Girard would be alerted and on his way. If it was removed the same. The weapons he carried consisted of a small-caliber automatic with a ten-shot magazine and an item perfected during the mugging epidemic towards the end of the last century; an apparent pen that fired anesthetic darts. And he also had his tongue and intelligence.

Celia was his main concern. Could Tagholm provide a cure?

The evidence was against it — if he could why was Victor Cruse still a zombie? Feyman remembered the events of the previous night and what Tagholm had said. A half-promise which he had left hanging. For effect or was he playing a devious game? Pretending to be drunk so as to throw straws into the wind and gauge the extent of potential gain. Certainly he was more than he seemed.

A moocher but one of a special breed. He'd worked as an engineer more recently than Girard had reported or the computers had known. Feyman wondered what other information they had lacked. What more he could gain.

Rising he stretched and examined the room he had seen only by a dim, blue light when helped to bed. It was as he expected; roughly finished, fitted with tiered bunks, some cabinets against a wall. A dormitory for any moochers who dropped by. Bunks for any workers who might be at the laboratory. Tagholm, absent, must have his own quarters.

He waved from a table as Feyman entered the dining room.

'Hi, there! How are you feeling?'

'Fair enough. You?'

'Hungry. Sit and eat.' He was hard, tough as all his kind had to be. He shrugged as Feyman shook his head.

'Please yourself.'

He wasn't alone. A handful of men sat at the far end of the table playing cards. Feyman recognized most of them but a pair were strangers. Keely was absent.

'He's taking a look outside,' said Tagholm when Feyman asked. 'A couple of the boys have gone with him. They'll be back soon.' He finished his coffee. 'Let's get to the lab.'

It was as they had left it. As Tagholm cleared away the bottles and glasses he said, 'Do you remember what we were talking about last night? After Keely joined us?'

'You were going to show me something.'

'I said I'd prove to you that I know what I'm talking about. The knowledge of the Old Ones isn't lost. It's waiting for us out there and I can find it. All it takes is money.'

Feyman said, 'You can have it on one condition — you give me what I need to cure my daughter.'

'I — '

'You haven't got it. All right. But you said you knew who had. Once it's mine I'll give you ten million. If you're wasting my time I'll be on my way.'

'Maybe.'

'You want to make an issue of it?'

'Relax.' Tagholm gestured with the flat of his hand. 'There's no need for sweat. Meet expenses, pay a bonus and things will be sweet all the way. You wanted to meet up with me and you have so where's the grief? I wasn't talking about you leaving — hell, you can go now if you want. It was the other thing. Maybe I can help you find a cure or maybe not. It'll cost to try. If you're willing to put up the backing I'll go ahead.' Tagholm added, as he saw Feyman's expression.

'Did I explain it all last night?'

'No.' The man was a moocher, a nut, but Feyman was here and had nothing to lose by listening. 'Put me in the picture.'

'You know what Kirlian photography is? Some call it aura-photography. You take a plate and put it against something and do things and you get an image. But the image you get isn't of the object itself though you see it in contrast. What you actually get is a picture of the aura surrounding it. The quick explanation is that you're recording the electrostatic field and, as usual, the quick explanation is wrong. You have to be getting more than that. For one thing you get an aura from a wide variety of substances and those auras are not the same. They should be if from a common surface-phenomenon but they aren't But, more important, there's something that baffles explanation if you're operating on a limited imagination. Take a leaf, break off a portion, and make a Kirlian image. The one you get is of an entire leaf.'

Tagholm came to a halt, confident he had said enough, but Feyman wasn't impressed.

'You get an image,' he corrected. 'A leaf is symmetrical in pattern and so are energy-fields. The aura is complete because it demonstrates that.'

'Limited imagination,' said Tagholm. 'I'm disappointed.'

'Why? Because I don't agree with you? I'm not trying to prove anything — you could be right for all I know. But take a magnet, cover it with a sheet of paper and scatter iron filings over the sheet. They will depict the magnet's energy-field. Chip a bit off the magnet and the image will be the same.'

Tagholm shook his head. 'You're missing the point. I've worked on Kirlian's for more than a dozen years now and I've checked out all the theories. I've improved the technique too — now it's strictly mine. I mentioned Kirlian photography only to put you in the picture. It was a start but I've left it way behind. And even if a field does generate a symmetrical pattern how can you have it both ways? Either the image is the result of surface-phenomena or it isn't. And, if it isn't, what do you have?' He supplied his own answer. 'You have a pattern frozen in time. The image of a thing which remains even though the original may have been broken or destroyed.'

Feyman looked around the laboratory. The litter on the benches was mainly of prefabricated circuits, many robbed of their chips, others enhanced by crude additions. The debris from the creation of what seemed to be heavy visors set in bulky helmets attached by wires to enigmatic boxes.

'Portable,' said Tagholm. 'Rough in places but they work. Suit-up and I'll give you a demonstration.'

To Feyman every part of the area surrounding the depot was the same but Tagholm saw things with a different eye.

'There!' His hand lifted to point at a jumble of stone. 'Artificial, see? It must have formed a part of a canal.'

If it had Feyman couldn't see it. The jumble was fairly regular, but so were others and rock tended to fissure along fracture lines in any case. A dozen other places could have been canals if that's all there was to go by, but Tagholm was a moocher and was skilled at reading sign.

'We'll set up on that knoll.' He waved to signal the others; four men carrying the equipment. 'The light's good and we should get a clear view.'

Of what he didn't say and Feyman

waited patiently until the man was ready.

'Here.' Tagholm lifted one of the helmets. 'This thing is heavy and takes a little practice to hold it steady. It helps to kneel. Just throw your weight back on your heels.' He lowered one of the bulky helmets over Feyman's own. 'Comfortable?'

'Yes.'

'Good. What do you see?' The view was as before, rugged ground, rocks, the dark bowl of the sky in which the sun blazed with eye-bright splendor. 'It'll change when I activate the helmet. I want you to understand what's going to happen. I've found a method of adjusting direct vision to the Kirlian level. Think of it as a fluoroscope against an x-ray. One's a living, moving picture the other a static photograph. And remember that what you see was actually there even if the original source is now only a pinch of dust. Ready?'

Feyman eased his legs a little. 'Yes.'

'Then here we go.'

For a moment there was nothing then the scene before Feyman's eyes began to change. Light dulled and detail blurred as if seen through mist or dirty glass. Lines and streaks of light that made a wavering pattern which, abruptly, fell into place.

Magic came into being.

Feyman saw a wall. There were blurs and scraps of fog and motes of darkness but there was no mistaking its structure. A tremendous edifice that ran in a straight line over the ochre plain. One made of giant blocks of stone neatly joined and smoothly rounded at the summit.

Carefully he turned his head. The helmet wavered but remained in place. He saw a flat expanse at the foot of the wall; an ancient canal where now rested jumbled shards. The flanking wall was either beyond the scope of the instrument or too far for him to see. The sky was lighter than it had been and it held tints of orange.

'Can you see it?' Tagholm's voice was excited over the wire. 'The wall? Can you see the wall?'

'Yes.'

'Proof, isn't it? There were canals in the

old days just as Lowell said. He must have been guided to reveal the truth. And Schiaparelli before him. They knew! They *knew!*'

Schiaparelli had called what he'd seen 'canali' an Italian word meaning channels. It had been Lowell who had insisted they must have been of artificial construction. Closer examination had failed to find any evidence to back either his theories or his observations. The canals simply did not exist.

Yet Feyman had seen a wall.

Could still see it and that flat expanse at its foot. Things that should continue behind him if the depiction was what Tagholm claimed it to be.

The helmet was heavy, precariously balanced; to gain a different viewpoint he would have to rotate his entire body. As he began to turn the image blurred, jumped, abruptly yielded to the normal scene of jumbled rock and dust and empty plain.

'Damn!' Tagholm was annoyed. 'The circuit's blown.'

'Can you fix it?'

'Not out here. I'll have to check it in the lab. But you saw it, didn't you? You saw it!'

Proof that the Old Ones had existed? That a mighty civilization had once ruled Mars? Or had it been just the bait for a con game?

Feyman thought about it on the way back to the depot. De-suited he watched as Tagholm began to inspect the equipment. The cases contained a power source, masses of electronic gadgetry, something that could have been an adapted computer.

'What you really saw,' explained Tagholm as he fussed over the components, 'was in the nature of an analogy. The scanners picked up the Kirlian effect, fed the data into the computer that extrapolated and condensed the information so as to pass it to the visual translators. It's like the old infra-red converters — they took the invisible radiation of heat and translated it to a visual frequency.'

'Then you don't really need the helmets.' Feyman touched one, lifted it, set it down again. 'We could have sat in here and watched everything on a screen.'

Tagholm glanced at him then concentrated on what he was doing. 'You know something about electronics?'

'A little. Where did you study?'

'The Hollendorph Insitute. I graduated in electronics and went on to study subspatial physics. Then the money ran out and I moved on.' Pausing he said, 'You're right about the screen but I haven't perfected the equipment enough for that yet. Mostly it's a matter of expense.'

And, more likely, one of salesmanship. Wearing the helmet had enhanced the occasion. It had given a feeling of involvement and immediacy that would have been lacking on a screen. But why had the equipment failed when he'd tried to turn?

Tagholm said, triumphantly, 'Got it! It was one of the adapted circuits and I guess I'm to blame. It isn't easy hooking up those chips. What I really need is a workshop and men to produce modules to order.'

And Feyman to pay for it. The pieces of

the con fell into place; the build-up, the demonstration, the equipment designed to fail when he'd tried to see too much. Now the sting. Once in he'd provide a gravy train for Tagholm, the Magus, even Keely. They had taken him for a gull and he felt a smoldering anger. Not at the attempt but at the waste of time. While they played their con game Celia still waited for a cure.

He said, 'Never mind your toys. Let's get to the real reason for my coming here. A cure for my daughter. You said you knew who could supply it. I want it. Ten million on delivery as I promised. When can I collect?'

'I can't be sure. A year, maybe two. It's hard to say.'

'What? Are you playing games with me?'

'No.' Tagholm backed from the murder in Feyman's eyes. Gesticulating, eyes wide, unnaturally bright he said, 'Christ, man, isn't it obvious? You saw the wall. You know who must have built it. The Old Ones existed just as the legends claim. How much proof do you need?

They were like gods. Gods! They had the answers to questions we haven't even thought of as yet. Secrets that have been lost in time. The answer to all problems is just waiting to be found. Once I've perfected my invention we'll be able to locate their vaults and discover their records. We'll learn all they ever knew. A cure for your girl — everything!'

'Is that the best you can offer me?'

'The cure is there. All you need is patience.'

'I haven't the time,' said Feyman — and pressed the button on his watch.

19

Furneaux was at Syrtis Parva and had bribed the desk to bell him of Feyman's return. From the screen he said. 'Max, I'm glad you're back. Any luck?'

'No.'

'We must talk. Your suite or mine?'

'Mine.'

'Give me ten minutes.'

'Make it later.' Feyman added, in explanation, 'I've just got in and I'm bushed.' A statement not wholly a lie; recent activity had been hard on pampered muscles. 'Say a couple of hours. Time for me to get a sauna.'

The masseur he chose was of his own kind; a man of around fifty, gray-haired, deft, one who wouldn't bother to offer more than his basic service. He grunted when Feyman, well-steamed, took the couch.

'We've a lot of tension here, sir.' His fingers probed and kneaded the muscles at the nape and shoulders.

'What you could do with is a few hours Russian.'

'No thanks.'

'I've the equipment here if you change your mind. Just slip on the headband, throw the switch and you go out like a light.' The fingers hadn't paused during the spiel. 'I'll guarantee you'll feel a new man when you wake.'

'No,' said Feyman again. The offer was tempting; micro-currents impinging on the sleep center of the brain to induce instant rest, but he hadn't the time. Why did men insist on running to their graves? 'Just the massage.'

He relaxed as the man fell silent and concentrated on his work. The steam had eased some of his tension and the massage would ease more but certain questions remained to bolster the rest. Why had Furneaux come to Mars? What was he after? Why had there been no message from Lynne?

He had sent her one of his own to update her on progress and had been disappointed that none had been waiting.

A disappointment sharpened by his physical need — odd how physical discomfort often induced sexual desire. But there had been nothing aside from Furneaux's call.

'Max!' The man hadn't waited. He smiled as he took the adjoining couch and waved aside the offer of a masseur.

'You will forgive me, I know, but you will understand my impatience.'

The smile was a mask as was the superficial charm. Had Feyman been in Russian sleep the man would have woken him but, in his place, Feyman would have done the same.

To his masseur he said, 'Thanks. That will be all for now.'

'Later, sir? There's still a lot to be done.'

'Maybe, I'll let you know.' As the man left Feyman said, 'I'll make it short, Jafek. Nothing.'

'You disappoint me.'

'Too bad but that's how it is.'

'I had hoped for more. Especially after the information you gained on Ganymede.' Pausing Furneaux added,

'That you obtained from Tara Riancon. I wondered why you had been so generous to her. A position found on Alpha 1. Money — what did she give you?'

'Some special papers Devin asked her to look after for him.' Feyman was curt. 'I guessed there had to be more than the stuff collected by your agent. I was right.'

'And?'

'As I told you, nothing. They were the figures on which he'd based his flight-plans for the deep dredges. Lynne checked them out on the way here. You can have them if you want — we know how good they are.'

'And Tagholm?'

'So you know about him. I'd gucssed as much. How long has it been since you trusted anyone?'

'A little longer than you — but that is because I was born earlier.'

Earlier and easier — Furneaux had started higher up the ladder, but he was as ruthless as any and more vicious than most.

Feyman said, 'You let me go ahead to gain what I could then you reckon you can move in and take it. Just like you've done with so many others. This time it's different. You may have sold Lynne the notion that you're a worried, doting parent, but I'm harder to convince.'

'You won't share the cure?'

'I'll share it. But first I have to find it — and I won't be pressured.' Feyman paused then added, 'As I told you so far there's nothing. Lars is a nut. He believes in the Old Ones and their legendary powers. Find their vaults and you have the answer to everything. I'm sorry. For you and me both. I'd hoped for more — but there it is. Another dead-end.'

But not a total loss. In the time he'd waited for Girard he'd made a deal with the man. The Kirlian images could be genuine or fake but either way they could lead to a fortune. If Tagholm had found a way of stimulating the visual areas of the brain it could lead to a new field of entertainment. The others, Keely and Quan Ki Nor, were in custody. The supplies hauled out to the depot had contained a quantity of machine-blasted stone; faked snowflakes to feed the tourist market. Counterfeiting was not tolerated on Mars.

Details and a revenge Feyman didn't mention to the other man.

'Nothing?' Furneaux drew in his breath. 'Max, we must work together. I have heard of a clinic that has been trying unusual methods such as the placing of chili powder on the tongue, shouting, bright flashes of light — you know of it?'

'It's all been tried. Celia had the entire program when I took her to Larrmah. That's in the Northern Territory, Australia. Doctor Mayne dug up some old data and gave it a whirl. The complete sequence; pain, pleasure, sensual stimulation, taste, touch, smell — it didn't work.'

'How about direct stimulation of various areas of the brain?'

'No. He was against that and I wouldn't have let him anyway. Play with the brain and you could wind up with a cabbage. When Celia's cured I want her whole.'

'As I with Saeed. But can we afford not to try? In the Belt there are many families to whom a zombie is a grinding burden.

Many of them would be willing to give permission for a new form of treatment.' He left the suggestion hanging. 'I understand Lynne is on Earth. Have you heard from her?'

'No. She's busy.'

'I know. She is checking her original findings. I have men doing the same. They were not optimistic and neither am I. I was hoping that you had found something, a clue — but you say you have not.'

'Don't you believe me?'

Furneaux hesitated then said, frankly, 'It isn't a matter of belief or even of trust. It is just that I must do everything in my power to help my son. As a father you can understand that.'

'Yes, Jafek, I know how you feel.' Feyman turned as an attendant touched his shoulder. 'What is it?'

'A taped message, sir. It is listed as urgent.'

The booth was in another room. Feyman went to it, listened, headed to where he had left his clothes. Furneaux intercepted him.

'Max! Your face! What is wrong?'

'I'm leaving for the Moon.'

'Now? But — '

'The message was from Wolfe,' snapped Feyman. 'Celia's doctor. Avril Kinski, her nurse, has zombied.'

*   *   *

She sat as they all sat; like a dead thing, a corpse, a dummy. One placed among an array of expensive furniture. The chair she occupied was thirty feet from her charge but they were closer now than ever before.

'How?' Feyman shook his head, recognizing the stupidity of the question. 'What happened?'

'She'd taken Celia out,' explained Wolfe. 'You knew we'd decided that the more exercise she had the better and there was always the possibility that something, anything, might induce a cure. Nurse Kinski had taken her to the Pinnacle and that's where it happened. Minchin was with them, thank God. He called me and I was with them ten minutes after Kinski zombied.'

'Where were you?'

'When he called? In the Stardust Bar.'

'Alone?'

'With a colleague. Tony Anholt. He — '

'I know about Anholt.' Furneaux was at his clinic now concerned as to the welfare of his son. 'So you were out drinking?'

'In my own time — no, your time. All of it is that. But everything was under control. You can check with Minchin as to that.'

An invitation he would accept and god help the doctor if he'd been careless. Feyman struggled to be calm. Nothing had happened to Celia. The basic situation hadn't really changed. Kinski had zombied but so had others. She had been close to Celia but that was probably coincidence. Why was Wolfe so concerned?

He gave the answer in one word. 'Contagion.'

'What? Impossible!'

'No.' The doctor was serious. 'I wish it was but it isn't. The possibility is there, Kinski was very close to Celia. She used to bathe her while they were both nude and there had to be a lot of skin to skin contact. I allowed it because it could have helped and was harmless.'

'So?'

'We could be dealing with either a mutated virus or something similar to leprosy. If the former we can expect a rush of new cases from those who have been in close or near, but prolonged contact. If the latter it isn't so bad. In the old days it was thought that leprosy was highly contagious and could be transmitted by secondary contact — a leper touched stone, you touched it afterwards, you caught the disease. We know now that leprosy is far less virulent than that but the old suspicion still clings.'

Feyman said, sharply, 'What are you saying? That close proximity could trigger the zombie reaction? Where is the proof?'

'There isn't any,' admitted the doctor. 'Kinski is the only evidence as yet and she presents only a possibility.'

One that would have to be checked. Lynne could do it, Furneaux too, and there was Anholt and his clinic — the attendants there would have been exposed to the danger if any existed. Feyman felt a sharp irritation; details, items, endless trivia — how could they help? If the thing was contagious then why no epidemic?

If it was contagious.

If it was a disease.

But, as Wolfe had hinted with his talk of leprosy, the mere suspicion of disease would be enough. Once people thought of zombiism as contagious panic would rule. Feyman had a vision of modern-day lepers, each kept in isolation, barely tended, a ghastly collection of the living dead — and Celia would be among them.

A probability and one that would have to be quashed. Medical opinion couldn't be that wrong. The affliction was just a condition of the mind, which stemmed from no apparent cause.

But why the nurse?

Wolfe must be wrong; it had to be coincidence. People went zombie so why not those in attendance on one? The odds would be — how to compute the odds? They had to be astronomical. Lynne would be able to supply the exact figure.

She looked at him from the screen of the phone. Her face, he noted, was drawn, revealing her fatigue. Signs that vanished as she smiled.

'Max! I'm glad you called! Too bad about what happened to Kinski.'

'Yes.'

'Celia?'

'The same. I'm with her now. Did you get the update on Tagholm?'

'I've fed it all into the computer but it's too soon for a final result.'

'That isn't why I'm calling. Can you run a secondary program?' He told her what he wanted. He was surprised by her reply. 'You've already run it?'

'Yes.' She glanced down as if to study some papers, looked back at him from the screen. 'First; the odds against someone on attendance to a zombie also becoming affected are so high against as to be meaningless unless there is definite evidence of contagion.'

'Is there?'

'No. There is a slight upcurve in the zombie-count due to reassessment of previous diagnosis. The increase is nothing like what would result from a recent mutation of any relevant virus. Wolfe was right to suspect the possibility but he doesn't have to worry about it.'

Feyman nodded, relieved but not wholly convinced. An epidemic had to start somewhere.

'The distribution?'

'Apparently random. Which is another reason against the condition being contagious.' She added, 'I'm sorry about Tagholm.'

'So am I.' The last hope gone — Feyman couldn't be philosophical about it. 'That damned computer! What made you run the secondary program?'

'Furneaux asked me to help out.'

'And you agreed?'

'Without telling you, yes.' Her eyes and voice were defiant. 'We made a deal; he let me use his men and facilities on Pallas. Two heads, Max, and I needed to save time.'

'Why?'

'Something odd. I've reframed the main program and am now running crosschecks. The answer should be along soon. When I have the final result I'll call and let you know.'

Feyman said, 'Why not bring it yourself?'

'Is that what you want?'

'You know damn well it is. I want to see you. I've missed you and, yes, that's what I want.'

'Good. I'll be with you as soon as I can.'

Which could be a few seconds ziptime, but she would have to reach the field and wait, and wait again for a landing and then get to him. And before that she would have to wait until the computer delivered its result. A long time — the way he felt a minute was too long.

20

Edmund Vladek was apologetic but firm. 'Please try to understand, sir. There is nothing personal about this. Your custom is appreciated but — ' The movement of his hands said it all.

'You want us out,' said Feyman. 'Right?'

'No, sir, not exactly.' The manager of the Armstrong was a diplomat as all hotel managers had to be. 'But the young woman who recently fell ill. There has been talk and some of the guests are worried. They fear a contagious illness. Ridiculous, of course, but there it is. And what with the extra nurses and equipment — ' Again he let his hands do the talking, 'Surely a hospital would be a more appropriate venue for the young lady.'

'Kinski,' said Feyman. 'Her name is Nurse Kinski.'

'Yes. So I understand. A most unfortunate occurrence.'

Vladek paused, waiting. 'Sir?'

A clever man, subtle, cunning. Not once had he mentioned Celia or hinted that the suite should be vacated. Instead he had concentrated his objection on the nurse. An employee, unimportant, expendable. Someone who, if ill, should be tucked away somewhere neatly out of sight. It's starting, thought Feyman, the taint of leprosy that Wolfe had mentioned.

He said, flatly, 'Do you realize that I could buy this hotel and put you on the street?'

'Yes, sir, I do.' Vladek met his eyes. 'But if you did that would you want your new manager to act any differently?'

'No,' admitted Feyman. 'I guess not.' Business was business and an investment had to show a profit. A system in which there was no place for charity. 'I'll take care of it,' he promised. 'Arrangements are already being made.'

Wolfe was making them. He sat before the phone, voice sharp, precise.

'I want Doctor Ivanych if you can get her — if not then the best pathological comparison expert you can. And I want a total-spectrum analyzer, the XHB 3562 if you can get it. Feyman's account. Have the machine and man zipped up here without delay. Anholt's clinic at Eratosthenes.'

He turned as the screen blanked to look at Feyman.

'Anholt won't like it but by the time we're installed it'll be too late for him to argue. I've arranged isolation facilities for Celia and Kinski. I'd like to retain our own nurses for control-checking. Right?' He continued as Feyman nodded: 'What I want to do is to make a wide-band comparison with various tissue and glandular exudations from the two women. Get right down to the molecular level. If we can find any unusual factor in common it might give us a clue.'

'Hasn't it all been done before?'

'Of course, but what were they making comparisons with? The DNA checked out and so did everything else but only in comparison with the normal pattern. This is the first time we've had two people zombie when they were close. If Celia did trigger the affliction in Kinski there could be traces. Wait too long and they may vanish. That's why I don't want to ship her to Earth. The zipdrive is a complication we can do without and we can operate quicker here. Anholt's clinic contains almost everything we need and he's willing to co-operate.'

Feyman nodded. Wolfe was calling the tune and it would be wrong to interfere. Minchin, seated, was in the outer room. He rose as Feyman approached leaving the book he had been reading lying open on the chair. A book of verse — the bodyguard was a man of unsuspected sensitivities.

'Sir?'

'Relax, Barry. Everything's all right.' Feyman glanced at the book. 'Whitman?'

'Fitzgerald. His translation of the Rubaiyat. I had it with me when Avril — Nurse Kinski — zombied. The first verse — you know it?' He continued as Feyman nodded, 'They've set up a new plaque in the Pinnacle and it seems appropriate. I wanted to check the wording.'

'Was it correct?'

'They'd changed the last line. The first three words. Instead of 'The Sultan's Turret . . . ' it now reads, 'The Lunar Pinnacle . . . ' More appropriate, perhaps, but it isn't quite the same.'

Was anything when forced into new clothes? Feyman said, 'Is that where it happened?'

'In the Pinnacle, yes. Avril had taken Celia up to the promenade and I waited as she led her along the edge, I checked the plaque but kept an eye on them both.' He added, bitterly, 'Not that it did any good.'

'You can't blame yourself.'

'Who else? I was there. I — ' His big hands closed into fists. 'Is there any hope?'

'If a cure can be found we'll find it,' said Feyman. 'Just where did it happen? You said Avril was leading Celia along the edge of the promenade,' he urged. 'How close?'

'Close,' Minchin frowned as he recalled the details. 'You could have touched the transparency by putting out your hand. The right hand — they were walking to

283

the left. Celia was ahead and Avril was just behind her. About five or six feet. I was moving towards them when it happened.'

'Tell me.'

'She just dropped.'

'No sound?'

'Nothing. If she hadn't started to fall I wouldn't have known anything was wrong. I got to her and then to Celia and got them both to a seat. I called the doctor and he arrived and took over.' Minchin added, bleakly, 'There was nothing I could have done. It all happened so fast. One second she was walking, smiling, alive. The next — it was just as if someone had thrown a switch.'

God perhaps?

Feyman said, 'We'll find the answer soon and the cure. You know about the move? Good. Keep your eyes open at Eratosthenes. Report anything you think I should know.'

A spy as well as a bodyguard but only a fool would neglect the obvious. Feyman strode from the suite, knowing there was nothing more he could do, angry with himself for the forced inactivity.

A man wanting answers.

One who could use a drink.

The Stardust Bar was too noisy, the Bowl too garish, the Mirror Room reflected his face in too many disconcerting angles. Feyman moved on, finding a small, dimly lit place at the edge of the main entertainment area. One with candles and the throb of barely audible music. A rendezvous for lovers, the air scented, quivering with whispers. The girl who approached him was tall, slim, her face an ageless mask beneath skillfully applied cosmetics.

'You are lonely?' She moved closer without waiting for an answer. Her gown was slit from hem to hip the gap revealing the long, smooth curve of her thigh. 'I may sit with you?'

'No.'

'But surely — '

'Just bring me a drink.'

It came in a tall glass frosted with a delicate pattern. A mixture of alcohols blended with a variety of fruit juices and ice. Feyman drank, ate some of the small cakes set on the table, signaled for another drink. Waiting he looked at the candle before him. A flame, guttering, what if he should blow it out?

Where would it go?

Like throwing a switch the bodyguard had said. Conscious awareness gone as if at the touch of a finger. An analogy used by Moynihan and Feyman leaned back as he brooded on the artist's words.

Where did a light go when you flipped the switch?

The second drink came and he killed it as he had the first. A third followed. As she brought the next the girl looked blank as he asked the question.

'Sir? I do not understand.'

'Never mind.' How would she know where a light went when you flipped the switch? How would anyone? 'Just bring me a drink.'

'You have one, sir. It is before you.'

'So it is. Bring me another.'

Feyman drank and studied the flame of the candle and drank again. A light; one instant it existed the next it didn't. Why? Where? How? The mechanics could be explained but talk of moving electrons and burning gases left something to be desired. Could a philosopher give the answer? Seeton, perhaps? If he asked his alien master what answer would he receive? Or would he merely add the question to the other?

Put two things together and what did you have?

Flip a switch and kill a light and what had you done?

What, exactly, had you done?

The clash of shattering glass jerked him to full awareness and he reared upright as the girl came quickly towards him.

'Sir? Is anything wrong?'

'No.' He'd been careless, knocking over his glass, spilling its contents over the table and the floor. The candle wavered as he looked at it, the face of the girl blurring as he felt the chair heave beneath him. The drinks had held an unsuspected potency. 'What are those things? What did you give me?'

'Zombies, sir,'

'What?'

'Zombies. It's the name of an old

287

cocktail.' She backed from his expression. 'Please! What is wrong?'

'Nothing.' He swallowed. 'Bring me some sobup pills. A treble dose. Water too.'

Ten minutes later he was sober and heading towards the Pinnacle.

It was a finger of rock thrusting upwards from the plain like the spire of an ancient cathedral. Hollowed, layered, the summit capped with a transparent dome. The topmost promenade was floored with a tessellation of black and silver the circular, central core striped in matching colors. From it to the edge was seventy feet of open space over which sightseers could stroll and gape at the vista beyond the dome. Earth, the stars, the empty bleakness of the lunar plain. Things the early astronauts had seen. Plaques commemorated their achievements.

Feyman searched until he found Gagarin's and halted to stand with his back to the core, eyes on the dome and the void beyond. Had the nurse been looking at the stars when she had been afflicted? At Minchin? At Celia?

He found and halted before the plaque that had held the bodyguard's interest.

Wake! For the Sun, who scattered into flight
The Stars before him from the Field of Night,
Drive Night along with them from Heaven, and strikes
The Lunar Pinnacle with a Shaft of Light.

The Persian poet wouldn't have liked the distortion of his work but, as Minchin had said, it was appropriate.

Feyman turned, gauging distance, looking at the outer edge of the promenade. Kinski must have stood about there and he moved to the position walking slowly, trying to emulate her movements. About an arm's distance from the transparency and she had walked to the left with Celia just ahead. Here? Here?

Nothing and, after a while, the tension eased from his stomach. How often did lightning strike in the same place?

Yet questions remained; had she sensed what was about to happen? A momentary premonition? There had been no scream, not even a sigh if Minchin was to be believed. Whatever the cause it had struck with swift and silent efficiency. A puff that had blown out the flame of a candle. The flip of a switch that had killed a light.

Feyman moved on around the circular promenade. As yet the main body of the complex was hidden from view on the far side of the Pinnacle. There would be lights and movement but here could be seen only cratered and shattered stone. Within the dome itself the light was a dusty blue doing little more than augment the external illumination but on the plain itself the Moon was silvered with starlight and Earthglow.

A sheen broken as he moved on the face of the complex; the nacreous glow broken by a flurry of brilliant motes of color from the identification lights of zipships newly arrived. He watched them, fascinated by the blinking, winking, ever-changing pattern. Gleams that flared and vanished to flare again like the glittering lights of a hypnotic lantern.

'Max!' He turned towards the voice. 'Max, is that you?'

'Lynne?'

She was a blur in the dim blue lighting, a figure that ran and, suddenly, was in his arms.

'Darling!' She hugged him close and he felt the yielding softness of her body, the hammering rhythm of her heart. As their lips parted she lifted a hand to touch his cheek, the fingers tender, caressing. 'Darling, it's been so long.'

Too long and the days since he had spoken to her last had seemed an eternity.

'It was quicker to zip than phone,' she said after they had kissed again. 'When I found the suite empty I thought you'd gone then I learned what had happened and came looking for you. I guessed you'd be here.'

'You could have waited. Had a shower or something.'

'I didn't know how long you'd be and I was in a hurry. Kinski?'

'Nothing new.'

'Celia?'

'The same.' He caught her by the elbows. 'Quit wasting time asking empty questions. Why were you in such a hurry?'

'Can't you guess?'

'I'm serious, Lynne.'

'I know, Max. I'm sorry.' She pulled herself free from his grip and walked to stare through the transparency before turning to rejoin him. Time to collect herself, he guessed. 'I — '

'Damn you — what is it?' His voice was sharp and attracted the attention of others. He ignored them as he closed the space between himself and the woman.

She said, dully, 'I finished the program. The revised update you wanted. I included all the latest data; Devin's death, the figures you got from his woman, the others Furneaux supplied, Moynihan, Tagholm, the lot.'

'And?'

'The computer delivered a name.' From her pocket she took a slip of paper but made no effort to hand it to him. 'A man who has the answer — according to the machine.'

'Give it to me.'

'Max, wait — '

'Give it to me!'

He snatched at the paper, tearing it from her hand, opening it to read the single name it contained.

His own.

21

The suite was too large; the empty rooms filled with ghostly memories, the mockery of laughter as Feyman poured brandy from a bottle. A drink that stung throat and mouth, and, somehow, failed to warm his stomach.

'Don't I get any?' Lynne held out a glass as he poured for the second time. 'Make it a big one.'

One as large as his own and he went through the ritual of drinking wondering at its purpose. To drink, to get drunk, to take pills to become sober, to drink again.

He said, 'Are you sure?'

'No.' She added, 'I'm sure the computer delivered your name but I'm not sure you have the answer you're looking for. How can I be?'

'Double-talk. You're covering your bets.'

'You want me to lie?'

'No, damn it, I want the truth but this

is crazy!' He looked at the glass he held and fought to be calm. 'That machine of yours says I have the answer — that I know how to cure Celia. If I could don't you think I would?'

'If you knew how, yes,' she agreed. 'Obviously you don't know. But the computer never said you had the cure — I didn't program it for that. The original names given, Tagholm and the others, were the results of me asking for someone who could provide the answer to what caused zombies. Once we knew that we could start hunting the cure.' She saw his frown. 'Let me give you an analogy. You know what colloid goitre is?'

'An abnormality of the thyroid gland leading to a pronounced swelling of the neck.'

'Yes. Now let's consider what a computer really is. Take two men. Both have a board before them punched with ten holes of various shapes and sizes. They have pegs to fit those holes. One man picks up a peg, tries it against each hole until he finds one that it'll fit, pushes it home. Then he does it all over again with each peg. The other man looks at the pegs, looks at the holes, determines which goes where and sets them in place. The first man is a computer. It can't really think. Not even the latest models with analog brains can do that. Not as we can. To find a solution it has to try every variable. Compared to a moron it's an idiot. Fast but that's about all. Understand?'

'What about the goitre?'

'Let's assume we don't know what causes it. We know it's there but that's about all. So we use a computer to provide the answer. It checks each and every case for associated details, factors, distribution. Distribution is easy and provides the clue all cases are inland away from the coast. Why?' Lynne shrugged. 'After about a million checks it's obvious that the coast-people have something the inland people don't. After another ten million we get the answer — inland people lack iodine. Once we know that we can provide iodine in salt and whatever and so prevent inland people getting colloid goitre.'

'So?'

'You're missing the point. At that time, while the search was being made, someone, somewhere probably knew the answer. A doctor or drummer or tramp. A rover or soldier or wanderer who had seen the people involved and had made the association.' Pausing she said, 'Someone who knew — but didn't know he knew.'

'Like now,' said Feyman. Then, 'Me?'

'The computer says so.'

'Damn the computer!' He looked at his hand, at the cuts left by the glass he had crushed, the blood mixed with the stinging brandy. 'If I know why the hell can't it tell me what I know? Why — ' He broke off as the phone chimed for attention. 'Yes?'

It was Minchin. He said, 'Sir, I think you'd better get over here. I heard the doctors talking and — '

'Celia?'

'I'm not sure but I heard talk of deterioration. Doctor Ivanych — '

'I'll be over. Tell no one.' As the screen died Feyman snapped, 'Lynne! Get your-self ready. We're going to Eratosthenes.'

'You get ready.' She pushed him from the phone. 'I'll make the arrangements while you dress that hand.'

He held it before him as the elevator dropped them to the lower levels. The cuts were minor, stinging beneath the transparent dressing, a discomfort that would quickly pass. As the journey down passed, the tube-trip to the local junction, the final stage in a roomy crawler.

Wolfe met them in the annex to the clinic. 'Max? Lynne?' His eyes held questions. 'Is anything wrong?'

'You tell me. Celia?'

'Stable as yet but — ' Wolfe broke off then added, bluntly, 'There are signs of deterioration. I wanted to make another check before letting you know. Doctor Ivanych is working on it now.'

'Take me to her.'

'I can't. Not yet. She's busy on — '

'Not the doctor, you fool! Celia!'

She lay on a bed beneath a plastic enclosure that almost filled the room.

A living person but one who looked too much like a corpse. The gown she wore was thin, blue, molding itself to the contours of her body. Her hands were lax, the fingers spread at her sides. Her eyes were closed the lashes silver smudges on her cheeks. A beauty, sleeping, waiting for the kiss that would restore her to life.

'I thought it best to put her in isolation,' explained Wolfe. 'A sterile environment. It probably is an unnecessary precaution but if the deterioration should accelerate her immunity-level could fall.'

He spoke as if there was no doubt as to the initial findings. Feyman said, 'How long?'

'Before we're certain?' Wolfe deliberately misunderstood the question. 'Doctor Ivanych has her own routine. She won't be hurried. It could be hours yet.'

More waiting, but in a place designed for those who could do nothing else there were distractions. Feyman looked at artificial flowers that moved, dolls cavorting in endless sarabands, frames containing images that shifted position at irregular intervals. He was alone. The geriatrics who normally would have used the room had been kept away by Anholt who also stayed discretely out of sight. Lynne, needing stimulation, had gone to ask him for drugs and the use of other facilities.

Feyman moved on, thinking, brooding. One wall held an area of constantly changing patterns of vivid colors, which caught and held the attention. Diffused it so that, after a while, the watcher seemed to be drifting in a universe of shimmering hues and intriguing shapes.

'Max?' Furneaux had entered the room. 'I heard.'

'Saeed?'

'As yet apparently the same but how to be sure? I would like to borrow your doctor to run similar tests. If — ' He broke off, swallowing, then said, 'If he also shows signs of deterioration then a decision will have to be made. I cannot just watch while he falls into decay. There must be another way. Cryogenics, per-haps. Have you considered it?'

Feyman nodded. 'The techniques haven't been perfected as yet. Fish, frogs, but that's about all. Freezing Celia would be like killing her. Even if she lived the cellular damage could make her worse than what she is now.'

'Then — ' Furneaux looked at the swirling patch of color then at his companion. 'Max, I must ask, I — '

'You know.'

'I — '

'You know the computer came up with my name. How? Lynne?'

'No. But once she and I spoke of money. I told her it was only as good as what it would do. It gained me information. Yes, Max, I know.'

A man who had used bribes and spies and wasn't ashamed to admit it. One too desperate to trust anyone and Feyman couldn't blame him for it. He would have done the same.

He said, 'The computer came up with my name, Jafek, that's true. But I don't have the cure. I don't even know the cause. God knows why the machine should think I have.' He added, seeing the doubt in the other's eyes, 'That's the truth. You can believe it.'

'But if the computer — '

'The machine says that I know,'

interrupted Feyman. 'The damned machine. But, if I do know, I don't know that I know.' He turned his head as the door began to open. 'That's Lynne. Ask her about it. She can explain.'

Lynne Colman wasn't alone. Behind her came Wolfe and Doctor Ivanych. She did the explaining.

'Max Feyman?' She was short, broad, as old as himself. 'I am Zelania Ivanych. I'm sorry but I have bad news.'

'The deterioration?'

'You know. Good. It helps.'

'I know it was suspected.'

'And has been confirmed.' She glanced at Wolfe then looked directly at Feyman. 'You may wish another opinion, of course, but it will only confirm my findings. Comparison-tests have shown a marked difference between the cellular tissue of your daughter and her nurse. I am speaking of relative viability. Samples taken from the spleen, liver, kidneys and ovaries leave no doubt. Catabolism has increased and will continue to do so at an increasing rate.' She paused then said, 'You understand what I am saying?'

'You are telling me my daughter is dying. I knew that. Now tell me how to save her.'

'I cannot. I do not have the information.'

Lynne said, 'But what went wrong? I thought that as long as she was taken care of Celia would continue as she is.'

'In some cases that could well be true but even so the ordinary life span cannot be anticipated. Once the higher intelligence ceases to function metabolic breakdown becomes an increasing probability. It varies with individuals, of course,' explained Ivanych. 'The cosseted and pampered seem to have less resistance. Men last longer than women and older women, those past childbearing age, last longer than those who are nubile. I merely report on observed data, you understand. The field still needs an in-depth investigation.'

Which would come far too late to do Celia any good.

Feyman said, harshly, 'How long?'

'Until she dies?' Ivanych shook her head. 'I cannot answer that with any degree of precision. If the deterioration progresses as I assume it will then she has only a matter of days. A week or two at the most.'

'Max!' Feyman heard Lynne draw in her breath, felt the clamping pressure of her fingers on his arm. 'Max — I'm so sorry!'

He said, 'Get on your machine. Find me the best information-retrieval expert in the world. Someone who knows how to tear the last secret from a living brain. Move!'

'Wait!' Ivanych looked at him, frowning. 'Maybe I can help. I have done work with amnesia-victims and have had experience in interrogating various criminal suspects. There are techniques — but why do you wish to use them?' She nodded as he explained. 'I understand. You know the answer but you have forgotten.'

'No!' Feyman's correction was explosive. 'I haven't forgotten. It's that — Hell, explain it Lynne. But later. In the meantime get what you need ready, Doctor Ivanych. Wolfe will help. How long?'

An hour, maybe two, time to zip to Earth to get unusual drugs. Time for Wolfe to make local arrangements. Time for Feyman to be alone.

He insisted on it; distractions were the last thing he wanted. Lynne faded away to keep Minchin company as he watched over Celia. Furneaux went to join his son. In the deserted part of the clinic Feyman wandered like a restless ghost.

One trying to remember.

It was useless. It wasn't as if he'd forgotten the title of a song, the spelling of a word or the word itself. A name, a face, an event. Things known but temporarily beyond the reach of the memory — the filing cabinet of the brain slow to yield the desired information. This was something he didn't even know he knew.

How to be sure that what he came up with was the truth?

Unless there was certainty everything could only be a guess. Maybe one of those guesses would be more than that but there was no way to be sure. But he had to be sure.

305

Celia's life depended on it.

He felt pain and looked down and saw the fingers of his clenched hand digging into the dressing, the wounds beneath. Pain he relished — while he felt it he was alive. And, living, could achieve.

'Max?' Furneaux came to join him. 'Ivanych is ready. Are you still of the same mind'

'Have I a choice?'

'There is always a choice.'

'Not for me. Not now.' Feyman drew in his breath. 'Let's get on with it.'

A chair had been placed before the area of shifting colored lights. Standing beside it Zelania Ivanych said, 'This will not be pleasant and could be dangerous. Had you merely forgotten something you knew and wished to remember it would be a simple matter of retrieval. If you had a secret you wanted to keep hidden there would be no problem either. But this — ' Her gesture was expressive.

'Can you do it?'

'I can try. In fact I won't be doing anything at all. The drugs I will give you are designed to temporarily abolish certain barriers within the mind. They will allow unhampered thought between the conscious and subconscious. Normally a thinking mind rejects what it considers to be illogical or unrelated or — but never mind that. Are you ready?' The sting of a hypodermic answered his nod. 'Relax now. Just sit and relax.'

Lie back and wait and look at the pretty colors and see how they change and change and change. Don't try to think or force memory or do anything but let the complex computer of the brain operate without brakes or preconceptions. Just lie and drift. Lie and stare. It was almost like going to sleep.

The pain hit like a bullet.

It smashed into his brain turning it into a swelling balloon, which pressed against the inner lining of his skull. Agony beyond his imagination and the universe dwindled to his skull, the pain that filled it, the torture that seemed as if it would never end.

Then came the light; vivid flashes as if lightning bolts were exploding before his eyes. The light, the pain, the sudden nausea as he felt himself begin to spin in a blurring montage of images.

Then the nightmare,

The delirium.

The coiling madness in which he lost identity and awareness.

Then, after an age, the glow of light and a face suspended before him.

'Here.' Zelania Ivanych held something beneath his nose and he gagged to the stench of acrid vapors. 'Your name,' she demanded. 'Tell me your name.' Her tone softened as he obeyed. 'Good. Breath deeply now. Deeply.'

More acrid stings and another face which replaced the doctor's. Furneaux who said, 'Max! Are you all right?'

'Yes.'

'And?'

'Yes,' said Feyman again. '*Yes!*'

22

The dome was a portable bubble set on a flat space some distance from where a finger of rock thrust itself towards the sky. Those inside wore suits, the helmets thrown back to allow of direct conversation, a better view of the summit of the spire. On it stood a man.

He was suited, strapped to a post, his figure slumped, dejected. A zombie close to death. The sound of his breathing echoed in a liquid gurgling from the speaker of the radio of his suit.

A guinea pig. The first zombie to be cured if Feyman was right. A martyr if he was wrong.

Furneaux paused in his restless pacing to listen to the radio, to stare at the man. He said, bleakly, 'The zipdrive caused that?'

'Yes.'

'You've no proof. Nothing.'

'It fits.' Feyman restrained his own

irritation. The other man lacked his own conviction. 'Why do you find it so difficult to accept? Because a ship is big and would smash anything it hits? But it doesn't, does it? Not when in zipdrive. It doesn't move, it's displaced, and if it travels at all as we know travel it does it in a different universe to our own. One moment it's here and the next there.' His finger made stabbing motions as he illustrated his point.

'But what if there's an effect we know nothing about?' he continued. 'A shock-wave, for example? It would travel with the ship and hit anything in the line of displacement. If it was a mountain, say, it wouldn't matter. Nor would it with metal or glass or air — but what about a human mind?'

'A brain? But — '

'Not a 'brain'!' Feyman was sharp. 'A brain is a physical organ and if it had been damaged we'd have spotted it. No zombie displays evidence of cerebral impairment. It isn't the brain that's affected but what it contains — the mind, the intelligence, the ego. The thing that makes a human being what it is. In a zombie it's gone. It's been blown away by the shock-wave of the zipdrive.'

Furneaux was stubborn. 'You've still no proof.'

'No, but how the hell do you suggest I get it? Turn a man into a zombie before your very eyes?' Feyman didn't wait for an answer. 'It fits,' he said. 'The figures bear me out. Lynne?' He looked to where she stood her eyes on the lonely figure on the spire. 'A random pattern, you said. Doesn't that support what I'm saying?'

She said, 'How much longer must he stay out there?'

A natural concern. The man hadn't been in place for long but, under stress, time dragged.

Into his radio Feyman said, 'Wolfe? How much longer?'

'Not long. The pilot's checking his alignment.'

'Team on standby?'

'Everything's as it should be. Just relax.'

Advice Furneaux should take. Feyman watched as the man paced, frowning, as tense as a coiled spring. A tension he both understood and shared.

'The mind shocked,' said Furneaux. 'Blown from the brain. It's almost past belief.'

'Try to see it,' urged Feyman. 'Just try.'

Feel as he had felt when his brain had boiled and the answer had come bobbing to the surface of his consciousness like a cork rising from the depths. Stand as he had stood on the summit of the Pinnacle and watch the ships as they zipped in and out. How often did they pass through the structure as they followed their line of flight? How close had he come to being hit?

Lynne had calculated the odds and they were small. The actual danger zone had to be both limited and brief for Kinski had turned zombie in the midst of a scattered crowd. The shockwave would last only a fraction of a second as it moved with the ship that had created it. A product of the drive that Zipadopalous had presented to mankind.

What did they say about Greeks bearing gifts?

'Wolfe?'

'Just about ready, sir.'

The pilot had heard and answered. 'On the count of five.'

A handful of seconds that stretched to seeming minutes. The pilot at his controls, the ship aligned on the solitary figure, the drive waiting the pulse that would zip it on its way. A giant bullet aimed at a tiny mote.

One that missed.

'What?' Feyman felt his stomach contract as he heard the report. 'Nothing? Are you sure?'

The zombie himself gave the answer; the liquid gurgle of his breath unbroken.

'Try again,' said Feyman. 'Take more time over your aim. You've got to send the heart of the drive through him. I told you that — through him!'

A guess — how could he be sure how the shockwave was generated? What form it would take? A tiny node, he'd assumed, but he could be wrong. Yet it had to be small and, logically, had to be on the line of flight. What had Tagholm said about Victor Cruse? The man had zombied while stooping over his model. The mind — how close must the shockwave be to affect the mind?

'The head!' Feyman yelled the order. 'Aim for the head!'

'Sir?'

'The head, damn you! Hit the head!'

Smash the brain with the impact of the zipdrive as had been done before. Shake it, jar it, force the intelligence to return. Flip the switch again to bring back the light.

Flip it and pray that Celia would live again.

'Mark,' said the pilot. 'Now!'

Nothing.

'Again!' Feyman felt sweat on his face, his neck. Perspiration that stung his eyes. 'Get the ship closer. Rig sights. Rest the subject's head against the hull if you have to but get that zipdrive on a line with his brain. Damn you — do it!'

'Max!' Lynne came towards him, her eyes anxious. 'The doctor warned you there could be after effects from those drugs she used.'

'Shut up!' He threw aside her hand.

'What are you waiting for out there?'

'Mark,' said the pilot. 'Now!'

Again nothing.

And again and again and yet again.

'It isn't going to work.' Furneaux was bleak. 'We're wasting our time.'

'Have you got a better use for it?' Feyman pulled at his collar as he struggled to breathe. 'Look at it this way,' he urged. 'A human is a flashlight with no obvious switch. No bump, no irregularity, no way of telling how to switch it off. God does that. He switches it on when you're born and it will shine as long as the batteries last or it remains intact. The zipdrive switched it off and we're trying to switch it on again. Trying,' he repeated. 'We don't know how. We can guess but we don't know. But, while we're fumbling around, the batteries are decaying. Soon, even if we learn the secret, it'll be too late. Celia will be dead. Can't you understand? My girl will be dead!'

'Mark,' said the pilot. 'Now!'

Another attempt, the ship vanishing to appear ninety-three hundred miles away. To zip back. To edge close, to align itself, the pilot failing but learning as he failed.

'Mark. Now!'

Moments that stretched to eternity and then, suddenly, came the voice. The blessed voice that babbled from the speaker that had only relayed a liquid gurgling.

'What's happened? Where am I? I feel ill. Help. Please, can anyone help me?'

'He's cured!' Wolfe shouted from the radio. 'By God, he's cured!'

Zelania Ivanych confirmed the statement. 'He is weak and needs extensive care but full bodily functions have been restored. His intelligence seems unimpaired. There was some initial confusion but that was due to a seemingly abrupt change of environment. When he zombied he was on a game park in Kenya.'

To find himself suddenly on the Moon — no wonder he had been confused. Feyman said, 'But he will be all right? There is no physical or mental damage?'

'None that I can observe.'

'Then we can go ahead and treat the others?'

'Why not? They cannot be worse than

what they are.' She added, 'But first I must take care of you. I warned about the drugs. You need sedation, monitoring and sleep.'

'Later.'

'After you have hallucinated? Suffered various physical discomforts? Made wrong decisions?' She added, impatiently, 'You have employed me because of my skill. Why are you so foolish as to ignore it?'

'I'm not but — '

'You have given your orders. Work is under progress. By the time it is accomplished you will be fit again — if you follow my instructions.'

Like his adoptive mother, firm in her orders, confident she knew best. But he still had trouble with his breathing and his heart raced and, too often, his vision was blurred or jarred with sudden flashes of light. The price paid for having dredged his memory or, more correctly, jumbling his stored and recorded data so as to achieve a desired result.

A good analogy — he must tell it to Lynne.

She was at his side when he woke. A

slim shape limned by the soft light of a window, the rich darkness of her skin enhanced by the soft folds of a white gown.

He said, 'I bet you want your ten million.'

'Of course.' If she was surprised at his waking she didn't show it. 'Did you think I was going to let you get away with it?'

'Do you honestly think you've earned it?'

'You tell me.' She moved to sit on the bed, one hand reaching to remove the band circling his skull. 'How do you feel?'

'Fine.' Drugs had calmed him and restored the natural rhythm of his body. Russian sleep had induced needed rest.

'How long?'

'Three days.' Her fingers touched his lips to still his protest. 'You needed every minute of it. And don't worry. Celia is fine and the work is finished.'

'Where are my clothes?'

'Relax.' She pressed him back against the bed. 'What about my ten million?'

'You'll get it but I still don't think you earned it.'

'No?'

'Think about it. The answers to your first program — how wrong could you get? Moynihan, Devin, Tagholm. Did they provide the cure?'

'We were looking for the cause, remember?' Her hand touched his cheek, his hair. 'But they helped.'

'How?'

She said, patiently, 'I've tried to teach you something about computers, Max. They're just machines. They work strictly on Aristotelian logic. Either a thing is or it isn't. Binary logic. Men aren't like that. They can and do use a wider range of concepts. A thing isn't just white or not white; it can be white some of the time or white as well as being something else. Remember Seeton? What he was asking you to discover was that no two objects can ever be identical and that there is more to a thing than the sum total of its parts. The relationship of items, for example.'

'Nothing is what it seems,' said Feyman. 'Right?'

'You're getting the idea. Remember the

319

question Seeton posed? What do you have when you place two items together? What, exactly, do you have? A computer would say you have two items, or one item of each of two classes, or one item of a class containing those two items. But a computer doesn't have imagination.'

'So?'

'Moynihan — remember what we discovered about him? A sculptor and an expert in guidance systems. One who knows all about curves and ballistics. Devin? Think of his experience with the zipdrive. His medical experience. If he could have been found in time and helped he could have supplied the answer.'

'Tagholm?'

'Can you say he didn't help?'

'No.' Feyman remembered the man and his concern with Victor Cruse. Why had he been so blind? 'He practically gave me the answer but I didn't realize it. When he talked about the zipdrive and the theory of a different universe. Of how they might have gone there. I thought he was talking about the Old Ones but, subconsciously, he could have been talking about zombies.'

'Scraps of information,' she said. 'And you remembered them all.'

'Is that why the computer came up with my name?'

'It was right, wasn't it, Max? You did have the answer and you did find the cure.' She rose from the bed, smiling. 'Come on, darling. It's time for you to get up.'

Outside all was ready. Feyman looked through a window at the heavy frame that cradled the ship. One of the smallest made now aimed like a missile at a dome set close. An umbilical tube connected the dome with the clinic and, within it, other frames would hold the patients in direct line with the zipdrive of the vessel.

Celia, Saeed, others — but Celia would be the first.

She came cradled in Minchin's arms looking frailer than he remembered and Feyman reached out to touch her. A gesture that turned into a caress as his fingers stroked the silver mane of her hair.

'Live,' he whispered. 'Live, my darling, live.'

'She will.' Lynne nodded and Minchin moved away. Heading for another chamber, the mouth of the umbilical tube, the dome beyond where Wolfe and Ivanych were already in position. 'Don't worry, Max. She's going to be all right. You know that.'

'I'll know it when I see it.' He had given the order for the ship, the frame, the dome, the entire set-up. Later the system would be refined. 'When I do we'll celebrate.'

But, now, he could only pray. Standing, waiting, listening to radioed instructions. Seeing the ship vanish. Hearing a voice that stung his eyes with tears of joy.

'Aldo? Aldo where — ' A pause then, 'What is this? Where am I? What's happened?'

Celia! Alive and well! Soon she would be herself again.

'Max!' Lynne gasped as he hugged and kissed her. 'What are you doing?'

'Telling you that I love you and want you with me for always. But, if you — '

'You're trying to be noble,' she interrupted. 'Don't. It's against your nature. Be hard and grasping and selfish and all the things you had to be in order to become as you are. You want me?'

'That's what I'm telling you.'

'Then I'm yours.' She smiled as he reached for her. 'Do we drink on it?'

'After we're married.'

'And then?'

'We go to Mars,' he said. 'To Titarus Sinus. Victor Cruse is there. Together we'll reach the stars.'

THE END

SWORD OF DAMOCLES

Sydney J. Bounds

After reports of strange occurrences are received from London, Paris and New York, Neil Vaughan is called to investigate. Gold, uranium and other precious metals are vanishing before the eyes of the men on guard. Vaughan is soon convinced that no human can be responsible, and that it's the work of some sinister outside force. And when Neil and his colleague Ann Delmar are abducted, they become entangled in a terrifying conspiracy that threatens to destroy the world.

THE FIVE MATCHBOXES

John Russell Fearn

After the police receive a warning of his impending murder, stockbroker Granville Collins is found shot dead in his office. The windows were closed, the door locked. The building was under police observation: no one except Collins entered, and no one left. And upon Collins' desk lay five empty matchboxes ... From this curious evidence Chief Inspector Garth of Scotland Yard is led not only to the cause of the murder, but also to a crime the Yard had labelled 'Case Uncompleted' ...

SHERLOCK HOLMES: THE GHOST OF BAKER STREET

Val Andrews

Taking the advice of Orson Welles, Greg Hargreaves leaves America for London, so escaping the attentions of Senator Joseph McCarthy. A 'B' movie scriptwriter, he arrives with a brief-case, overnight bag and his typewriter. Soon he is looking for accommodation — and notices a familiar address in the classified adverts of a newspaper. Taking the rooms in Baker Street he becomes involved in murder and mystery as he discovers them to be haunted — by the ghost of Sherlock Holmes . . . ?

DEATH OF A COLLECTOR

John Hall

It's the 1920s. Freddie Darnborough, popular man about town, is invited to a weekend at Devorne Manor. But the host, Sir Jason, is robbed and murdered hours after Freddie's arrival. However, one of the guests is a Detective Chief Inspector. An odd coincidence? The policeman soon arrests a suspicious character lurking in the shrubbery. But Freddie alone believes the man to be innocent. And so, to save an innocent man from the gallows, Freddie himself must find the real murderer.

SHERLOCK HOLMES AND THE GIANT'S HAND

Matthew Book

Three of the great detective's most singular cases, mentioned tantalisingly briefly in the original narratives, are now presented here in full. The curious disappearance of Mr Stanislaus Addleton leads Holmes and Watson ultimately to the mysterious 'Giant's Hand'. What peculiar brand of madness drives Colonel Warburton to repeatedly attack an amiable village vicar? Then there is the murderous tragedy of the Abernetty family, the solving of which hinges on the depth to which the parsley had sunk into the butter on a hot day . . .

EXCEPT FOR ONE THING

John Russell Fearn

Many criminals have often believed that they'd committed the 'Perfect Crime', and blundered. Chief Inspector Garth of Scotland Yard is convinced that modern science gives the perfect crime even less chance of success. However, Garth's friend, scientist Richard Harvey, believes he can rid himself of an unwanted fiancée without anyone discovering what became of the corpse. Yet though he lays a master-plan and uses modern scientific methods to bring it to fruition, he makes not one but several mistakes . . .